"Wh

"I'm impressed," Khalil said with a condescending smile. "Any other woman would be begging for mercy—"

"If that's why you've abducted me, you're out of luck."

"I'm sorry to disappoint you, Joanna, but I took you because I can use you."

"Use me? I don't understand...."

Khalil's smile changed, took on a darkness that made her breath catch, and his gaze moved over her lingeringly. "Don't you?"

SANDRA MARTON has always believed in the magic of storytelling and the joy of living happily ever after with that special someone. She wrote her first romantic story when she was nine, and fell madly in love at sixteen with the man she would eventually marry. Today, after raising two sons and an assortment of furry, four-legged creatures, Sandra and her husband live in a house on a hilltop in a quiet corner of Connecticut.

SANDRA MARTON

Hostage of the Hawk

Harlequin Books

TORONTO • NEW YORK • LONDON
AMSTERDAM • PARIS • SYDNEY • HAMBURG
STOCKHOLM • ATHENS • TOKYO • MILAN
MADRID • WARSAW • BUDAPEST • AUCKLAND

ISBN 0-373-11780-9

HOSTAGE OF THE HAWK

First North American Publication 1995.

CHAPTER ONE

THE cry of the *muezzin* rose in the warm evening and hung trembling over the crowded streets of Casablanca. Joanna, listening from the balcony of her hotel suite, felt a tremor of excitement dance along her skin. Not that there was really anything to get excited about. While the hotel was Moroccan in décor, it was the same as hotels everywhere.

Still, she thought as she put down her cup and leaned her crossed arms on the balcony railing, it was wonderful to be here. This part of the world was so mysteriously different from the life she knew. She felt as if she had stepped back in time.

'Jo!'

Joanna sighed. So much for stepping back in time. Her father's angry bellow was enough to bring her back to the present with a bang.

'Jo! Where in hell are you?'

And so much for the mystery of Casablanca, she thought as she straightened and turned towards the doorway. She was used to Sam Bennett's outbursts—who wouldn't be, after twenty-six years?—but she felt a twinge of sympathy for whatever poor soul had made him this angry. Jim Ellington, probably; Sam had been on the phone with his second in command, which meant that Jim must have done or said something that displeased him.

'It's about time,' he snapped when she reached the bedroom. 'I've been calling and calling. Didn't you hear me?'

5

'Of course I heard you.' Her father was glaring at her from the bed where he lay back against a clutch of squashed pillows, his ruddy face made even redder by the pain in his back and his bad temper. 'Half the hotel must have heard you. I take it there's a problem?'

'You're damned right there's a problem! That stupid Ellington—he screwed things up completely!'

'Well, that's no surprise,' Joanna said pleasantly. She plumped the pillows, then took a small vial from the nightstand and dumped two tablets into the palm of her hand. 'I tried to tell you not to rely on him, that he was the wrong person to deal with this idiotic Eagle of the East.'

'Hawk,' Sam said grumpily as he took the tablets from her. 'Prince Khalil is called the Hawk of the North.'

'Hawk, eagle, east, north—what's the difference? It's a stupid title for a two-bit bandit.'

Sam grimaced. 'That "two-bit bandit" can end Bennettco's mining deal with Abu Al Zouad before it starts!'

'That's ridiculous,' Joanna said. She poured some orange juice into a glass and offered it to Sam. 'Abu's the Sultan of Jandara——'

'And Khalil's been harassing him for years, stirring up unrest and trouble whenever he can.'

'Why doesn't Abu stop him?'

'He can't catch him. Khalil's as sly as a fox.' Sam smiled grimly, then gulped down the juice and handed back the glass. 'Or as swift as a hawk. He swoops down from the northern mountains——'

'The mountains Bennettco wants to mine?'

'Right. He swoops down, raises hell, then escapes back to his mountain stronghold, untouched.'

'He's more than a bandit, then,' Joanna said with a little shudder. 'He's an outlaw!'

'And he's opposed to the deal we've struck with Abu.'

'Why?'

'Abu says it's because he's opposed to our bringing in Western ways.'

'You mean, he's opposed to our bringing in the twentieth century,' Joanna said with a grimace.

'Whatever. The point is, he'll do everything he can to keep Bennettco out. Unless we can change his mind, we might as well pack up and go home.'

'I still don't understand. Why can't Abu simply have Khalil arrested and——?' Her brows lifted as her father began to chuckle. 'Did I say something funny?'

'Have him arrested!' Sam's laughter grew, even though he clutched at the small of his back. 'Have pity, Jo! It hurts when I laugh.'

'I'm not trying to amuse you, Father,' Joanna said stiffly. 'I'm just trying to understand why this man isn't in prison if he's an outlaw.'

'I told you, they can't catch him.'

Joanna's brows lifted. 'In case you haven't noticed,' she said drily, 'Khalil can be "caught" this very moment at a hotel on the other side of Casablanca.'

'Yeah, yeah, I told that to Abu.'

'Well, then——'

'He doesn't want to cause an international dispute with the Moroccan government. This is their turf, after all.' Sam sighed and fell back against the pillows. 'Which brings us back to square one and that dumb ass Ellington. If only I could get out of this bed long enough to make that dinner meeting——'

'When we left New York, you made it sound as if this meeting were pro forma.'

'Well, it is. I mean, it should have been—if I hadn't pulled my back.' Sam's mouth turned down. 'I know I could have finessed the hell out of Khalil—and now Ellington's managed to make a bad situation worse.'

'I'll bet Ellington obeyed you to the letter, phoned your regrets about tonight's meeting, and said he'd dine with Khalil in your place.'

'You're darned right he obeyed me.' Sam glared at her. 'If he wants to keep his job, he'd better!'

'It's what everybody who works for you does,' Joanna said mildly, 'even if your orders are wrong.'

'Now, just a minute there, Joanna! What do you mean, my orders were wrong? I told Ellington to tell the Prince that something had come up that I couldn't help and——'

'You insulted him.'

'What?'

'Come on, Father! Here's this—this robber baron with an over-inflated ego, gloating over the fact that he's got Sam Bennett, CEO and chairman of the board of Bennettco, over a barrel. He's probably been counting the minutes until tonight's meeting—and then he gets a call telling him he's being foisted off on a flunky.'

'Don't be foolish! Ellington's my policy assistant.'

'It's a title, that's all, and titles are meaningless.' Joanna sat down on the edge of the bed. 'Who would know that better than an outlaw who calls himself a prince?'

'I already know we're in trouble, Jo! What I need is a way out.'

'Take it easy, Father. You know what the doctor said about stress being bad for your back.'

'Dammit, girl, don't fuss over me! There's a lot at stake here—or have you been too busy playing nursemaid to notice?'

'I am not a "girl".' Joanna got to her feet, her gaze turning steely. 'I am your daughter, and, if you weren't so determined to keep me from knowing the first thing about Bennettco, I wouldn't have to ask you all these questions. In fact, I might have been able to come up with some ideas that would have gotten you off the hook tonight.'

'Listen, Jo, I know you have a degree in business administration, but this is the real world, not some ivy-covered classroom. It's Ellington who let us down. He——'

'You should have told Ellington to tell Khalil the truth, that your back's gone out again.'

'What for? It's nobody's business that I'm lying here like an oversized infant, being driven crazy by you and the hotel doctor!'

'Contrary to what you think,' Joanna said coolly, 'being sick isn't a sign of weakness. Khalil would have understood that he wasn't being insulted, that you had no choice but to back out of this meeting.'

Sam glared at her, then shrugged his shoulders. 'Maybe.'

'What did you plan on accomplishing tonight?'

'For one thing, I wanted to eyeball the bastard and see for myself what Abu's been up against.'

'And what else?'

Sam grinned slyly. 'He may resent us dealing with Abu—but I bet he won't resent a deal that has some under-the-table dollars for himself in it.'

A frown creased Joanna's forehead. 'You mean, Bennettco's going to offer him a bribe?'

'*Baksheesh*,' her father said. 'That's what it's called, and you needn't give me that holier-than-thou look. It's part of doing business in this part of the world. It just has to be done delicately, so as not to offend the s.o.b.' Sam sighed deeply. 'That was the plan, anyway—until Ellington botched it.'

'Have you any idea what, exactly, he said to the big pooh-bah?'

'To Khalil?' Sam shook his head. 'Ellington didn't even talk to him. He spoke to the Prince's aide, a guy named Hassan, and——'

'His first mistake,' Joanna said with crisp self-assurance. 'He should have insisted on speaking with the Prince directly.'

'He tried, but Hassan says Khalil doesn't deal with underlings. Underlings, can you imagine?' Sam chuckled. 'The only good part of this is imagining Ellington's face when he heard that.'

'What did Ellington say then?'

'The conversation was all Hassan's after that. He made some veiled threats, said if Sam Bennett wasn't interested enough to deal with Khalil man to man, Khalil wouldn't be responsible for what might happen.'

'That's insane! He can't be fool enough to think he can ride down on our crews with his band of cut-throats—can he?'

'Maybe—and maybe not.' Sam grunted with displeasure. 'Hell, this meeting was the key to everything! I just know that if I could have met face to face with this Khalil I'd have been able to convince him that Bennettco——'

'We still can.'

'How? I just told you, Khalil won't meet with Ellington.'

'But he might meet with me,' Joanna blurted.

She hadn't planned those words, but once she'd said them her heart began to pound. Sam's prideful stubbornness, Ellington's blind adherence to orders and the arrogance of a greedy bandit with a fancy title had set in motion a series of events that might make all the difference in her life.

Sam laughed, and Joanna looked up sharply.

'Right,' he said sarcastically. 'I'm supposed to send my daughter to meet with a barbarian. Do I look like I'm crazy, Jo?'

'Come on, Father. He's not exactly a barbarian. Besides, I'd be meeting him for dinner, in a fancy restaurant. I'd be as safe as if I were dining in my suite.'

'Forget it. The great Khalil doesn't deal with underlings.'

'Maybe he'd feel differently about someone named Bennett, someone with a vested interest in Bennettco.' Joanna looked at her father, her voice strengthening as her idea took shape. 'Someone who could identify herself as not just her father's daughter but Bennettco's vice-president.'

Sam scowled darkly. 'Are we back to that?'

'We never left it. Here I am, your only offspring, somebody who grew up as much in the field as in the office——'

'My first mistake,' he grumbled.

'Here I am,' Joanna said evenly, 'the only person who knows as much about business as you do, my university degree clutched in my hand, and you absolutely refuse to let me work for you.'

'You do work for me. You've been my hostess in Dallas and New York since you were old enough to carry on a conversation.'

'That,' she said dismissively.

'Yes, that! What's wrong with "that", for lord's sake? Any girl in her right mind would grab at the chance to——' Joanna's brows lifted and Sam put his hand to his heart. 'Forgive me,' he said melodramatically. 'Any *woman* in her right mind would be perfectly happy to——'

'Stanford Mining's offered me a job,' Joanna said softly.

'They did what?'

She walked to the bureau and leaned back against it, arms folded over her breasts. She'd never meant to tell her father about the offer this way; she'd planned on working up to it, using it as the final link in a well-conceived argument designed to convince him, once and for all, that she wanted more than to be a beautifully dressed figurehead, but she knew in her bones that now was the moment.

'The manager of their Alaskan operation is leaving. They asked if I might be interested.'

Sam's face darkened. 'My own daughter, working for the competition?'

'The key word is "working", Father. I've told you and told you, I've no intention of spending the rest of my life like some—some over-age débutante.'

'And I've told you and told you, I didn't work my tail off so my daughter could get her hands dirty!'

'I'm not asking you to let me work in the field,' Joanna said quickly. 'Even I know better than to expect the impossible.'

'Joanna.' Sam's voice softened, took on the wheedling tone she knew so well. 'I need you doing just what you've been doing, baby. Public relations is important, you know that. Having your name listed on the committee for charity benefits, getting your picture in the paper along with the Whitneys, Rockefellers and Astors——'

'You're wrong about the importance of that stuff, Father, but if it matters to you so much I can hold down a job and still manage all the rest.'

Sam gave her a long, hard look. 'Are you serious about taking the job with Stanford?'

Until this moment, she had only been serious about considering it—but now she knew that she would accept the offer rather than go on playing the part her father had long ago assigned her.

Joanna nodded. 'Yes,' she said, her eyes locked with his, 'I am.'

They stared at each other while the seconds passed, Joanna's emerald gaze as unwavering as her father's pale blue one, and finally he sighed.

'Do you really think you could get this guy Khalil to agree to meet with you?'

A little thrill raced through Joanna's blood but she was careful to keep her expression neutral.

'I think I could have a good shot at it,' she said.

'By telling him you're my daughter?'

'By telling him the truth: that you're ill but that this meeting is too important to miss. By telling him I'm your second in command, that everything I say has your full support and backing.'

Sam pursed his lips. 'That simple, hmm?'

Nothing was ever that simple, Joanna knew, not in business, not in life, and surely not in this place where custom vied with progress for dominance. But this was no time to show any hesitation.

'I think so, yes.'

She waited, barely breathing, while Sam glowered at her, and then he nodded towards the phone.

'OK.'

'OK, what?' Joanna said, very calmly, as if her pulse weren't racing hard enough so she could feel the pound of it in her throat.

'Call the Prince's hotel. If you can get past that watchdog of an aide, if Khalil will talk to you and agree to meet with you in my place, you've got a deal.'

Joanna smiled. 'First let's agree on the terms.'

'I'm your father. Don't you trust me?'

'You're my father and you raised me never to sign anything without reading it twice.' She saw a glimmer of a smile in Sam's eyes as she held up her fisted hand. 'Number one,' she said, raising her index finger, 'I get a vice-presidency at Bennettco. Number two, it's a real job with real responsibilities. Number three——'

Sam threw up his hands. 'I know when I'm licked. Go on, call the man. Let's see if you're as good as you think you are.'

Joanna's smile blazed. 'Just watch me.'

Her father reached out, took a notepad from the nightstand, and held it out to her. 'Here's the phone number. It's direct to Khalil's suite.'

Joanna nodded and reached slowly for the phone. She would have preferred to make this call from the other room instead of here, with her father watching her every move, but Sam would be quick to pounce on that as a sign of weakness.

'Good evening,' she said to the operator, then read off the number on the notepad. Her stomach was knotting but Sam's gaze was unwavering and she forced a cool smile to her face as she sank into the bedside chair, leaned back, and crossed her legs. The phone rang and rang. Maybe nobody was there, she thought—and at that moment, the ringing stopped and a deep voice said something in a language she couldn't understand, except for the single word 'Hassan'.

Joanna clasped the phone more tightly. 'Good evening, Mr Hassan,' she said. 'This is Joanna Bennett. Sam Bennett's daughter.'

If Hassan was surprised, he covered it well. 'Ah, Miss Bennett,' he said in impeccable English, 'I am honoured. What may I do for you?'

'Well?' Sam said impatiently. 'What's he saying?'

Joanna frowned at him. 'How are you enjoying your stay in Casablanca?' she said into the phone.

'The city is delightful, Miss Bennett, as I'm sure you agree.'

Joanna touched the tip of her tongue to her lips. 'And the Prince? Is he enjoying his stay, as well?'

'Dammit,' Sam hissed, 'get to the point! Is Khalil there, or isn't he?'

'Indeed,' Hassan said pleasantly, 'my Lord Khalil has always had a preference for this city.'

Joanna took a deep breath. Enough pleasantries. It was time to get down to business.

'Mr Hassan,' she said, 'I should like to speak with the Prince.'

Hassan's tone hardened. 'I'm afraid that is out of the question, Miss Bennett. If you have a message for him, I shall be happy to deliver it.'

Joanna's hand began to sweat on the phone. Her father was still giving her that same steadfast look and a self-satisfied smile was beginning to form on his lips.

'Give it up, baby,' he said quietly. 'I told you you couldn't pull it off.'

'Mr Hassan,' Joanna said evenly, 'I'm afraid you don't understand. I want to assure the Prince that the only reason for the change in plans is because my father is ill. As for Mr Ellington—I'm afraid he misunderstood my father's instructions. The Prince will be dining with my father's representative, whom he trusts completely and holds in the highest esteem.' Joanna looked at Sam. 'Vice-president Jo Bennett.'

'One moment, please, Miss Bennett,' Hassan said.

Joanna felt a rush of hope. She smiled sweetly at Sam. 'He's going to put the Prince on,' she said, and hoped that her father couldn't see her crossed fingers.

*   *   *

Across town, in the elegant royal suite of the Hotel Casablanca, Prince Khalil glared at his prime minister.

'What sort of man is this Sam Bennett,' he growled, 'that he asks his daughter to telephone me and beg on his behalf?' He folded his arms across his chest, his dark blue eyes glinting like sapphires in his tanned, handsome face. 'Bennett is worried,' he said with satisfaction as he leaned his hard, six-foot frame against the wall.

'Precisely, my lord. He must be ready to bend to your will or he would not have ordered a woman to act as his agent.'

'Only a fool would bring his daughter on such a trip,' Khalil said with disdain. 'The woman must have thought Casablanca would be an exotic playground in which to amuse herself.'

Hassan's grizzled brows lifted. 'Of course, my lord. She is, after all, of the West.'

Khalil grunted in assent. 'What does she want?'

'To speak with you.' Khalil laughed and Hassan permitted himself a smile. 'I told her, of course, that was not possible, and then she said Sam Bennett wishes tonight's dinner meeting to take place.'

'Ah.' Khalil's hard mouth curled with the shadowy beginnings of an answering smile. 'Bennett has decided he wants to keep our appointment now?'

'He is ill, sire, or so the woman claims, and wishes to send an emissary. I suspect it is an excuse he uses to save face.'

Khalil strode forward. 'I do not meet with emissaries, Hassan.'

Hassan dipped his head in respect. 'Of course, my lord. But her offer is interesting. The emissary is Joe Bennett, a vice-president of the company.'

Khalil's eyes narrowed. 'Who? I have never heard of such a person.'

Frowning, Hassan took his hand from the telephone and spoke into it. 'We have no knowledge of this person who would meet with Prince Khalil, Miss Bennett. Is he related to your father?'

'Mr Hassan, if I could just speak with the Prince——'

'The Prince does not speak with underlings, and he surely does not meet with them,' Hassan said coldly. 'If you wish to answer my questions, I will transmit the information to my lord. Otherwise, our conversation is at an end.'

'Jo,' Sam said, 'give it up. You're not gonna get to first base with this guy.'

Joanna swung away from her father. 'Jo Bennett is hardly an underling, Mr Hassan.'

'Jo,' Sam said, his voice gaining authority, 'did you hear me? Give it up. You took a shot and you lost.'

'Miss Bennett,' the voice in her ear said sharply, 'I asked you a question. Who is Joseph Bennett? Is he Sam Bennett's son?'

Joanna swallowed, shut her eyes, then opened them. 'Yes,' she said into the telephone, praying that the Prince would forgive the deception after she convinced him that there'd be enough money in this deal to make him happy, 'yes, that's right, sir. He is.'

'A moment, please.' Hassan put his hand over the mouthpiece again and looked at the Prince. 'The man you would dine with is the son of Sam Bennett.'

Khalil glared at his minister. 'A son,' he snarled, 'a young jackal instead of the old.' He stalked across the elegant room, turned, and looked at Hassan. 'Tell the woman you will accept a meeting with her brother. Perhaps my judgement is wrong. Perhaps the son has some influence on the father. At any rate, you can convey my message clearly: that I will not be ignored in this matter!'

Hassan smiled. 'Excellent, my lord.' His smile fell away as he tilted the phone to his lips. 'Miss Bennett.'

Joanna blinked. 'Yes?'

'I, Adym Hassan, Special Minister to His Highness Prince Khalil, will meet with your brother tonight.'

Joanna clutched the cord tighter. 'But——'

'Eight o'clock, as planned, at the Oasis Restaurant. As they say in your world, take it or leave it, Miss Bennett.'

'Jo?' Sam's voice rose. 'Dammit, Jo, what's he saying? He's turning you down flat, isn't he?'

Joanna hunched over the phone. 'Of course,' she said, 'eight o'clock. That will be fine. Thank you, sir.' She hung up the phone, took a deep breath, and turned to her father. 'You see?' she said briskly. 'That wasn't so hard after all.'

'He's meeting with you?' Sam said doubtfully.

Joanna nodded. 'Sure. I told you he would.'

Sam blew out his breath. 'OK,' he said, 'OK. Now, let's figure out how to get the most mileage we can out of tonight.' He looked at his daughter and a grin spread over his face. 'Not bad, kid,' he said, 'not bad at all.'

'It's not "kid",' Joanna said with an answering smile. 'It's Vice-President Jo Bennett, if you don't mind.'

Vice-President Joseph Bennett, she thought, and gave a little shudder. Things were going to get interesting when Special Minister Adym Hassan found out he'd been lied to.

Halfway across the city, Special Minister Hassan was already thinking the same thing.

'I am suspicious of Bennett's motives, my lord,' he said to Prince Khalil as he hung up the phone. 'But we shall see what happens. The woman's brother will meet with me tonight.'

Khalil nodded. 'Good.' He turned, walked slowly across the room, and stood gazing out the window as if he could see beyond the city to the hills that marked the boundary of his kingdom. Sam Bennett was a sly, tough opponent; it was more than likely his son would be the same. Too sly and too tough for Hassan, who was loyal and wise and obedient but no longer young. How could he let the old man meet with Bennett? If he'd learned one thing these past weeks, it was that dealing with anybody named Bennett was like putting a ferret in charge of the hen house.

Khalil spun away from the window. 'Hassan!'

'Yes, my lord?'

'I have changed my mind. I will meet with Sam Bennett's son myself.'

Hassan looked startled. 'You, sir? But——'

'There are no "buts", Hassan,' Khalil said sharply. 'Call down for some coffee and lay out my clothing.' He smiled tightly, the sort of smile that chilled those who knew him well. 'I promise you this, old man. One way or another, tonight will change everything.'

It was Joanna's thought, too, as she sat beside her father, only half listening as he droned on about tonight's agenda.

One way or another, she knew in her bones that her life would not be the same after this night ended.

Afterwards, she would remember how right she'd been.

CHAPTER TWO

WHAT did you wear to a dinner meeting with a Hawk of the North?

Not that she'd be dining with the great man himself, Joanna thought wryly as she peered into the wardrobe in her bedroom. Her appointment was with Hassan, Special Minister to Prince Khalil, although what a bandit needed with a minister was beyond her to understand. Their conversation had been brief but it had been enough to give her a good idea of what he'd be like.

He'd be tall and angular and as old as the hills that lay beyond the city. The skin would be drawn across his cheekbones like ivory papyrus. His eyes, pale and rheumy with age, would glitter with distaste when he saw her and realised that she was Joanna Bennett, for he lived in a world in which female equality was unheard of.

Joanna smiled tightly as she riffled through the clothing hanging inside the wardrobe.

How would she convince him to continue the meeting, once her deceit was obvious?

'Surely, the great Khalil wishes prosperity for his people,' she'd begin, 'and would not wish you to refuse to meet with someone who can provide it.' Then, as distasteful as the prospect was, she'd dig into her purse, take out the envelope with the numbered Swiss bank account her father had established, and slide it gently across the table.

After that, Hassan wouldn't care if she were a man, a woman or a camel.

* * *

Joanna glanced at her watch as she stepped from her taxi. Eight o'clock. Her timing was perfect. She put her hands to her hair, checking to see if the pair of glittery combs were still holding the burnished auburn mass back from her face, then smoothed down the skirt of her short emerald silk dress. She'd hesitated, torn between a Chanel suit and this, the one cocktail dress she'd brought with her, deciding on the dress because she thought the suit might make her look too severe, that it would be enough of a shock for the minister to find himself dealing with a woman without her looking like *that* kind of woman.

The doorman was watching her enquiringly and she took a deep breath, lifted her chin, and walked briskly towards him. She was nervous but who wouldn't be? Everything she wanted—her father's approval, the vice-presidency at Bennettco—hung on the next couple of hours.

'*Masa el-kheyr*, madam.'

Joanna nodded. 'Good evening,' she said, and stepped through the door.

Soft, sybaritic darkness engulfed her, broken only by the palest glow of carefully recessed overhead lighting and flickering candlelight. Music played faintly in the background, something involving flutes and chimes that sounded more like the sigh of wind through the trees than anything recognisable to her Western ear.

'*Masa el-kheyr*, madam. Are you joining someone?'

The head waiter's smile was gracious but she wondered if he would continue smiling if she were to say no, she wasn't joining anyone, she wanted a table to herself.

'Madam?'

Joanna gave herself a little shake. The last thing she needed was to get herself into an antagonistic mood.

'Yes,' she said pleasantly. 'My name is Bennett. I believe there's a reservation in my name.'

Was it her imagination, or did the man's eyebrows lift? But he smiled again, inclined his head, and motioned her to follow him. There was an arched doorway ahead, separated from the main room by a gently swaying beaded curtain. When they reached it, he drew the curtain aside and made a little bow.

'The reservation request was for as private a table as possible,' he said.

Joanna nodded as she stepped past him. A private alcove. That would be better. At least, she and Hassan wouldn't have to deal with——

A man was rising to his feet from the banquette. Joanna's eyes widened. He was thirty, perhaps, or thirty-five, tall, with a lithe body and broad shoulders contained within a finely tailored English suit. Her gaze flew to his face. His eyes were shockingly blue against his tanned skin. His nose was straight, his mouth full and sensuous. And he was smiling.

Joanna's heart gave an unaccustomed thump. Lord, he was gorgeous!

She smiled back, flustered, then turned quickly to the head waiter.

'I'm terribly sorry, but there must be an error.'

'Yes.' The man had spoken, and she looked back at him. His smile had grown, tilting a little with intimacy and promise. 'I'm afraid the lady is right.' His voice was soft, smoky, and lightly tinged with an indefinable accent. 'If I were not expecting a gentleman to join me——'

The head waiter cleared his throat. 'Excuse me, sir. I believe you said you were waiting for a Mr Joseph Bennett.'

'Yes, that's right. I am.'

'Then there's been no error, sir. This is the gentleman—uh, the lady—you were waiting for.'

Joanna's eyes flew to the man's face. They stared at each other in silence. This was Hassan, Minister to Prince Khalil? Oh God, she thought, as she saw his expression go rapidly from surprise to disbelief to fury, and she stepped quickly forward and shot out her hand.

'Mr Hassan,' she said with a big, determinedly cheerful smile, 'what a pleasure to meet you. I'm Jo Bennett.'

He looked at her hand as if it were contaminated, then at her.

'If this is an example of Western humour,' he said coldly, 'I should warn you that I am not amused.'

Joanna swallowed, dropped her hand to her side, and fought against the desire to wipe the suddenly damp palm against her skirt.

'It's not a joke, no, sir.'

Sir? *Sir*? What was going on here? Was she really going to permit this—this arrogant minister to a greedy despot to reduce her to a deferential schoolgirl? It was one thing to be nervous, but it was quite another to let the balance of power be stripped from her without so much as a whisper. Whether Mr Hassan liked it or not, they were here on equal footing. The sooner she reminded him of that, the better.

Joanna lifted her chin and forced a cool smile to her lips.

'I am Joanna Bennett,' she said calmly. 'And I can understand that you might be a bit surprised, but——'

'Where is Sam Bennett's son?'

'I'm his son.' Joanna shook her head. 'I mean, he has no son, Mr Hassan. I am——'

'You are his daughter?'

'Yes.'

'You are Joe Bennett?'

'Joanna Bennett. That's right. And——'

He swung towards the head waiter. 'Bring me the bill,' he snapped. 'For my apéritif, and for whatever the restaurant will lose on this table for the evening.' He snatched a liqueur glass from the table, drained its contents, slammed it down, and made a mocking bow to Joanna. 'Goodnight, Miss Bennett.'

Open-mouthed, she stared after him as he strode towards the beaded curtain, still swaying delicately from the waiter's exit, and then, at the last second, she stepped out and blocked his path.

'Just a minute, Mr Hassan!'

'Step aside, please.'

It was the 'please' that was the final straw. The word was not offered politely, but was, instead, tossed negligently at the floor, as one might toss a bone to a dog. Joanna drew herself up.

'And what will you tell Prince Khalil, Mr Hassan?' Joanna slapped her hands on her hips. 'That because you were narrow-minded, old-fashioned, petty and stupid——'

The dark blue eyes narrowed. 'I advise you to watch your tongue.'

'And I advise you to use your head,' Joanna said sharply. 'Prince Khalil sent you here to meet with me.'

'I came here to meet with Sam Bennett's son.'

'You came to meet with his emissary, and that is precisely what I am!'

A muscle knotted in his cheek. 'Whose idea was this subterfuge? Ellington's? Or was it your father's?'

'There was no subterfuge meant, Mr Hassan.'

His smile was swift and chill. 'What term would you prefer? Deception? Trickery? Perhaps "fraud" has a finer ring.'

'At the worst, it's just a misunderstanding.'

He rocked back on his heels and folded his arms over his chest. 'Please, Miss Bennett, don't insult me with games of semantics.'

'I'm simply trying to explain why——'

'What sort of misunderstanding could possibly have led to your thinking I would even consider discussing your father's greedy plans for my country with you?'

His disdain, his contemptuous words, were like a bucket of iced water. Joanna met his harsh gaze with unflinching directness.

'Wrong on all counts, Mr Hassan. For starters, I did not wish to discuss anything with you. It was Prince Khalil I wished to meet this evening, remember? As for greed—it is not my father who's standing in the way of progress and betterment for the people of Jandara, it's your high and mighty ruler.'

Hassan's brows lifted. 'An interesting description of the Prince, Miss Bennett. Clearly, your father didn't send you on this errand because of your subtlety.'

Joanna knew he was right. Her words had been thoughtlessly spoken but to back down now would be a mistake.

'He sent me because I have his trust and confidence,' she said. 'And if my honesty offends you, I can only tell you that I see little value in not being as direct as possible.'

An unpleasant smile curled across his mouth. 'How readily you use the word "honesty"—and yet here you stand, having lied your way into my presence.'

'I did no such thing! I am who I said I was, Jo Bennett, the vice-president at Bennettco.'

'And we both know that if you had identified yourself properly, this meeting would not have taken place.'

'Exactly.' Joanna smiled thinly. 'I'm glad you admit it so readily. You and the Prince would have turned your noses up at the very idea of discussing business with a woman.'

'Typical Western nonsense,' he sneered. 'A woman, taking a man's name, trying to pretend she can do a man's job.'

'I haven't taken anything,' Joanna said coldly. ' "Jo" is short for Joanna. As for a woman trying to pretend she can do a man's job—I don't know how to break this to you, but women don't have to "pretend" such things any more, Mr Hassan. In my country——'

'Your country is not mine,' he said, his tone rife with contempt.

'It certainly isn't. In *my* country——'

'In Jandara, those who lie do not break bread with each other.'

Joanna glared at him. 'It isn't my fault you assumed Jo Bennett was a man.'

'I don't recall you attempting to correct that assumption, Miss Bennett.'

Anger overcame her. 'If I didn't,' she said, stepping forward until they were only inches apart, 'it was because I knew your boss would react exactly the way you are at the prospect of a woman representing Bennettco. No wonder my father's gotten nowhere all these weeks! Trying to deal with a—tyrant is like—like . . .'

The rush of words stopped, but it was too late. He smiled slyly as she fell silent.

'Please, Miss Bennett, don't stop now. You've called Prince Khalil a tyrant, a chauvinist—I can hardly wait to hear what else you think of him.'

What was she doing? She'd come here to further her cause, to succeed in a tricky endeavour and convince Sam that she was capable of carrying her weight at Bennettco, and instead she was alienating the Hawk of the North's right-hand man with terrifying rapidity. She took a deep breath, let it out, and pasted a smile to her lips.

'Perhaps—perhaps I got carried away.'

The Prince's emissary smiled tightly. 'You may not be given to subtlety but you surely are given to under-statement. Referring to m—to the Prince as a dictator is hardly——'

'I never called him that!'

His brows lifted. 'But you think it.'

'Certainly not,' she said, lying through her teeth. Of course she thought it. If this—this overbearing, ar-rogant, insolent pig of a man was the Prince's minister, she could only imagine what the Prince himself must be like. 'Besides, my opinion of your Prince is no more important than your opinion of me. You and I have lost sight of the facts, Mr Hassan. We are representatives, I of my father, you of Khalil. I doubt if either of them would be pleased if we reported back that we'd cancelled this meeting because we'd gotten off to a bad start.'

Her smile did nothing to erase the scowl from his face. 'Perhaps we'll simply tell them the truth, that we can-celled it because I resent having been made a fool of.'

He had a point. Much as she hated to admit it, she had twisted the facts to suit her own needs. She'd lied to him, lied to her father. And if Sam found out ...

'Well?' She blinked. He was staring at her, his ex-pression as unyielding as stone, his eyes cold. 'What do you say to that, Miss Bennett?'

'I say... I say...' Joanna swallowed hard. Go for broke, she thought, took a deep breath, and did. 'I say,' she said, her eyes meeting his, 'that you have every right to be annoyed.'

His scowl deepened. 'The start of another bit of trickery?'

Colour flared in Joanna's face but she pressed on. 'I admit I may have stretched the facts, but I haven't lied. I do represent my father. I have his every confidence and I'm fully authorised to act on his behalf. I know you have a problem dealing with me, but——'

But, he thought impatiently, his eyes on her face, but! She was good at suggesting alternatives, this Joanna Bennett. She had insulted him, apologised to him, and now she was doing her best to convince him her father had Jandara's best interests at heart—but for what reason? Why had Sam Bennett sent her? She kept insisting she was Bennettco's representative, but what man would be fool enough to believe that?

His gaze moved over her slowly, with an insolence born of command. She kept talking, although her skin took on a rosy flush, and that amused him. Why would a woman like this colour under his gaze? Surely she was not innocent? She was a beauty, though, perhaps more beautiful than any woman he'd ever seen. What she couldn't know was that her beauty meant nothing to him. Despite what Joanna Bennett thought she knew of him— or of the man she believed him to be—he had long ago wearied of beautiful faces and bodies that hid empty souls. He preferred his women with strength and character, individuals in their own right, not the pampered lapdogs Western women so often were.

The logical thing to do was to tell her that she and her father had wasted their time, that he was not Hassan but Prince Khalil, that he was not interested in whatever game it was they were playing.

But if he did that, he would not learn what game it was. And that, surely, was vital.

'I still fail to see why your father sent you to this meeting, Miss Bennett,' he said sharply, 'unless he thought you could succeed where others had failed simply through the element of surprise.'

'If it makes you feel any better,' Joanna blurted, 'I'm as surprised as you are. I thought you'd be—I thought...'

'Yes?' His eyes narrowed. 'What did you think?'

Joanna stared at him. That you'd be a million years old, she thought, that you'd be a wizened old man... His voice. His voice had sounded old on the telephone. Hadn't it? Maybe not. She could remember little of their conversation except how desperate she'd been to make him commit to this meeting—this meeting that she was on the verge of ruining, unless she used her head.

'I thought,' she said carefully, 'we'd be able to sit down and discuss our differences face to face.'

He smiled tightly. 'But not man to man.'

'The bottom line,' Joanna said, ignoring the taunt, 'is that we—that is, Prince Khalil and Bennettco—*do* have differences.'

'Yes. We do, indeed.' His voice hardened. 'Bennettco thinks it can ignore Khalil and deal only with Abu——'

'Abu Al Zouad is the King of Jandara,' Joanna said with an icy smile, 'or has your Prince forgotten that little item?'

'He is not the King, he is the Sultan,' Khalil said sharply, 'and surely not Khalil's.'

'Abu is the recognised leader of your country, and he has guaranteed Bennettco the right to mine in the northern mountains.'

Khalil's smile was wily. 'If that is the case, why has your father sent you to meet with me?'

'To talk about what is best for Khalil's people.'

He laughed, this time with such disdain that it made Joanna's spine stiffen.

'You spout nonsense, Miss Bennett. That is hardly the issue we're here to discuss.'

At least the man was blunt, Joanna thought grimly. 'Very well, then,' she said. 'My father's sent me to talk about what will most benefit Bennettco—and what will most benefit your Prince, which is why your unwillingness to listen to what I have to say surprises me, Mr Hassan. This meeting is in Khalil's best interests, but——'

'Sir?' They both spun towards the curtained doorway. The head waiter was standing just inside it, smiling nervously. 'The bill, sir.'

Khalil looked at the silver tray in the man's hand, then at Joanna. She was right. It would be foolish of him not to find out what tricks her father had up his sleeve, even if it meant enduring her company.

'Very well,' he said. 'I will give you an hour, and not a moment more.'

Joanna nodded. She was afraid to breathe or even to answer for fear this impossible man would change his mind again and walk out.

Khalil nodded, too, as if they had made a pact, then looked towards the waiter.

'Bring us the meal I ordered,' he said with a dismissive wave of his hand.

'Certainly, sir.'

'Be seated, Miss Bennett.'

Be seated, Joanna thought as she slid into the padded banquette, just like that. No 'please', no attempt at courtesy at all. It was ludicrous. He'd already ordered dinner, even though she'd reserved the table. The man was impossible, arrogant and imperious and——

'So.' She looked up. He had slid into the booth opposite her and he was watching her intently, his eyes unreadable as they met hers. He sat back, his broad shoulders straining just a bit at the jacket of his suit, and a faint smile touched his mouth. 'Why don't you start our meeting by telling me about the Bennettco project?'

She did, even though she was certain he knew all the details. It would only help her make her case at the end, when it became time to ask him for assurance that he'd not try and hinder the project. She talked through the lemon soup, through the couscous, through the chicken baked with saffron, and finally he held up his hand.

'Very interesting—but you still haven't told me why I should permit—why my Prince should permit Bennettco to mine in the mountains?'

'Well, first of all, the operation will bring money into Jandara. It will—it will...' Joanna frowned. 'Permit, Mr Hassan? I don't think that's quite the correct word, do you?'

'English is not my first language, Miss Bennett, but I learned it at quite an early age. "Permit" was the word I intended.'

'But the decision's not Khalil's. It's Abu's.'

'Is it?' He smiled lazily. 'If that were completely true, you wouldn't be here.' He smiled lazily. 'You're concerned that Khalil will interfere with the project, isn't that right?'

What was the sense in denying it? Joanna shrugged her shoulders.

'We think he might try, yes.'

'And have you stopped to consider why he might do that?'

'Perhaps he hasn't given enough thought to how much this project will benefit his people.'

The arrogance of the woman! Khalil forced his smile not to waver.

'He is selfish, you mean?'

Joanna looked up, caught by the man's tone. He was still smiling, but there was something in that smile that made her wary.

'Well, perhaps he doesn't see it that way,' she said cautiously, 'but——'

'But you do, and that's what matters.'

'You're twisting my words, Mr Hassan.'

'On the contrary. I'm doing my best to get to the heart of your concerns. What else am I to tell him, apart from a warning about his selfishness?'

Joanna stared at him. Was he asking her to be more direct about the bribe money? It galled her to make such an offer but reason seemed to be failing. Sam had warned her that this was the way things were done in this part of the world, but——

'Don't lose courage now,' he said coldly. 'Be blunt, Miss Bennett. It's why you came here, remember?'

'Tell him—tell him we won't tolerate any harassment of our workers.'

'I see. You worry he might have them beaten. Or shot.'

There was a lack of emotion in his words, as if having men hurt were an everyday occurrence.

'We are not "worried" about anything, Mr Hassan,' she lied, her tone as flat as his. 'This project will go ahead, no matter what your Prince does. We simply want to encourage Khalil's co-operation.'

His nostrils dilated. He yearned to take the woman's slender shoulders in his hands and shake some sense into her.

'Really?' he said, and if Joanna had not been so caught up in her own determination to succeed, if she had not already decided that the only thing that would close the deal was the enormous bribe Sam had suggested, she'd have heard the note of warning in that single word. 'And how are you going to do that, Miss Bennett?'

Joanna gave him a look laced with contempt, then unclasped her evening bag and took out the envelope her father had given her.

'With this,' she said bluntly, and slid the envelope across the table towards him.

He bent his head and looked at it. His anger made the words on the paper a meaningless blur but then, what this female Judas was offering didn't matter. She had accused him of being obstinate, selfish and despotic, and now she had sought to buy him off as if he were a common thief.

'Well?' Her voice was impatient. 'Is it enough?'

Khalil silently counted to ten, first in Arabic, then in English, and then he took the envelope and stuffed it into his pocket.

'Oh, yes,' he said, the words almost a purr, 'it is enough. It is more than enough.'

She'd done it! She'd won the co-operation of the infamous Prince Khalil—well, Bennettco's bribe had won it, which stole away most of the pleasure. Concentrate on the victory, she told herself, on what this will mean to your future...

He rose to his feet. 'Come, Miss Bennett,' he said softly.

Joanna looked up. He was holding out his hand and smiling. Or was he? His lips were drawn upwards, but would you really call what she saw on his handsome face a smile?

'Come?' she said, smiling back hesitantly. 'Come where?'

'We must celebrate our agreement with champagne. But not here. This place is for tourists. I will take you somewhere much more authentic, Joanna.'

Joanna? Joanna's heart thudded. Don't go with him, she thought suddenly, don't go.

'Joanna?'

That was ridiculous. She had done it, she had closed the deal her father thought couldn't be closed. What on earth could there possibly be to fear?

Smiling, she got to her feet and gave him her hand.

He led her through the restaurant, pausing only long enough to say something to their waiter, who bowed respectfully all the way to the front door. Outside, the night seemed to have grown darker. He was holding her elbow now, his grip firm, as he led her towards a low-slung sports car at the kerb.

Suddenly, Joanna thought of something.

'Did you say we were going to have champagne?'

He nodded as he handed her into the car, came around to the driver's side, then slipped in beside her.

'Of course. It's a celebration. Why do you sound surprised?'

Joanna frowned slightly. 'Well, I'm just—I guess I *am* surprised. I didn't think your people drank wine.'

He smiled. 'Believe me, Joanna,' he said, 'you are in for a number of surprises before the evening ends.'

He stepped hard on the accelerator and the car shot into the night.

CHAPTER THREE

EVERYONE Joanna knew had had the same reaction to the news that she was going to Casablanca.

'Oh,' they'd sighed, 'how incredibly romantic!'

Joanna, remembering the wonderful old Humphrey Bogart-Ingrid Bergman movie, had thought so too. But after a week she'd decided that things must have changed a lot since the days of Rick and Ilse. Casablanca was ancient and filled with history, it was beautiful and mysterious, but it was also the economic heart of Morocco which meant that in some ways it was not only prosaic, it was downright dull.

The man beside her, though, was quite another story. She gave him a surreptitious glance from beneath her lashes. There was nothing dull about him. She'd never met a man like him before, which was saying a great deal. The circles in which she travelled had more than their fair share of handsome, interesting men but even in those circles, this man would stand out.

Joanna's gaze flew over him, taking in the stern profile, the broad sweep of his shoulders, the well-groomed hands resting lightly on the steering wheel. He seemed so urbane, this Mr Hassan, so at home in his well-tailored suit, his pricey car, and yet she could easily imagine him in a very different setting.

Her lashes drooped a little. Yes, she thought, she could see him in her mind's eye, dressed in long, flowing robes, mounted on a prancing black stallion, racing the wind across the desert under a full moon.

'You're so quiet, Miss Bennett.'

Joanna's eyes flew open. They had stopped at a light and he was looking at her, a little smile on his lips. For some reason, the thought that he'd been watching her without her knowing made her uncomfortable. She sat up straighter, smoothed her hair back from her face, and gave him a polite smile in return.

'I was just enjoying our drive,' she said.

She glanced out of the window as the car started forward. They were passing the Place des Nations Unies, deserted at this hour except for a solitary pair of strollers, a man and woman dressed in traditional garb, she walking barely noticeable inches behind. Like a respectful servant, Joanna thought with a grimace, or a well-trained dog...

'She is not being obedient, Miss Bennett,' the man beside her said, 'she's simply gawking at the sights.'

Joanna swung towards him. He was looking straight ahead, intent on the road.

'I beg your pardon?'

'That couple.' He glanced at her, an insolent smile curled across his mouth. 'You were thinking the wife was following her husband out of custom, but I assure you, she wasn't.'

He was right, but what did that matter? Joanna gave him a frigid look.

'Do you make a habit of reading people's thoughts, Mr Hassan?'

'It isn't difficult to read yours. You seem convinced we classify our women as property in this part of the world.'

She smiled tightly. 'Your definition, not mine.'

He laughed. 'A diplomatic response, Joanna—but then, your father would not have sent you on such a delicate mission if he hadn't been certain of your ability to handle yourself well.'

Some of the tension flowed from Joanna's posture.
He was right. This *had* been a delicate mission, and she'd
carried it off successfully. Let the Hassans and Khalils
of this world have their *baksheesh* and bribes. What did
it matter to her? She'd set out to snatch success from
the jaws of defeat and she'd done it, despite the arrogant
high-handedness of the man next to her.

'You're quite right,' she said pleasantly, folding her
hands neatly in her lap and watching as the dimly lit
streets spun by, 'he wouldn't have.'

'He has no sons?'

'No.' Her smile grew saccharine sweet. 'I know you
must think that makes him quite unfortunate, but——'

'I suspect it simply makes him all the fonder of you.'
He glanced at her, then looked back to the road. 'You
must be very important to Sam Bennett, not only as vice-
president of Bennettco but as the jewel of his heart.'

Joanna looked at him. She was neither, she thought
with a little pang, not the vice-president of Bennettco
nor even the jewel of her father's heart. It was Bennettco
itself that was his love, it always had been, but now that
she'd pulled this off...

'Am I right, Joanna?'

She swallowed. 'Yes,' she said quickly, 'I'm as important to him as you are to Prince Khalil.'

His head swung towards her. 'As I...?'

'I mean, you must be very important to Khalil, for
him to entrust you with negotiating such important
matters.'

'Ah.' He smiled. 'Of course. You are wondering if my
word is Khalil's bond.'

'No. I wasn't. It never occurred to me to doubt——'

'I promise you, he will abide by my judgement.' He
looked towards her, and suddenly his smile fled. 'I will
not repudiate anything I do this night.'

Joanna's brows rose a bit. 'I'm sure you won't,' she said politely.

The man wasn't just arrogant, he was contemptuous as well. '*I will not repudiate anything I do this night*'! It was almost laughable. How could he say that when he was only the Prince's minister?

Khalil would be even worse, Joanna thought with a sigh, rigid and imperious and completely egotistical. It was probably a good thing he hadn't agreed to meet with her. As it was, she'd had difficulty holding her temper with Hassan. Heaven only knew how she'd have been able to deal with someone even ruder.

But she didn't have to worry about that any more, she thought, permitting herself a little smile. She'd done the impossible, pulled the coup that would set her firmly on a path she'd always wanted, and if she'd have been happier managing it without pushing a bribe under Hassan's nose, well, so what? If that was how things were done here, who was she to ask questions? She had succeeded, and now she and Hassan were going to drink a toast to their agreement.

Joanna settled back in her seat. Where was he taking her, anyway? Somewhere far from the streets she knew, that was obvious. In fact, they'd left the streets behind completely. The car was racing along a straight, narrow road that disappeared into the night.

Perhaps he was taking her to some place less Western than the restaurant where they'd dined. Perhaps, for all his seeming urbanity, he'd been uncomfortable in its sophisticated setting.

'You've become quiet again, Joanna.' Hassan stepped down harder on the accelerator and the car seemed to leap forward. 'Have you nothing to say, now that you've got what you wanted from me?'

His tone was nonchalant but Joanna sensed the underlying derision in his words. She shifted into the corner of her seat and smiled politely.

'I think we've each gotten something from the other,' she said.

'Of course. You have my promise of co-operation and I——' He looked at her, his teeth showing in a swift smile. 'I have the bribe you offered me for it.'

It was what she had just been thinking but hearing it from the man on the receiving end made it different. Surely people who demanded you buy them off didn't go around admitting it, did they? And, just as surely, they didn't make it sound as if *you* were the one who'd done something vile—yet that was what his tone had clearly suggested.

Joanna caught her bottom lip between her teeth. Was he still smarting over the clumsy way she'd handled the bribe offer? She knew she hadn't done it with any subtlety, that she'd come within a breath of insulting him, something that was not done anywhere but especially not in this part of the world.

'Everyone benefits,' he said softly. 'Khalil is bought off, Bennettco turns a handsome profit—and Abu Al Zouad grows fatter.' He looked at her, his eyes unreadable in the darkness. 'All in all, a fine arrangement, yes?'

Joanna shifted uneasily. 'Look,' she said, 'I don't know what it is between your Prince and the Sultan, but——'

'Everyone benefits,' he said again, his tone hardening. 'Everyone—except my people.'

As if he or his mighty Prince really gave a damn, she thought angrily. But she bit back the words and offered ones that were only slightly more diplomatic instead.

'It's too late to have second thoughts, Mr Hassan. You gave me your word——'

'If you intend to speak to me of honour,' he said coldly, 'you are wasting your time.'

Their eyes met and held. All at once, Joanna wished she were anywhere but here, in this fast car tearing through the darkness to some unknown destination.

'I was only going to point out that we agreed on——'

'What would you have done if I'd turned down your bribe money?'

'Listen, Mr Hassan, if you've a problem with Prince Khalil's accepting money...' Joanna clamped her lips together. What was needed here was a touch of diplomacy, not anger. 'I wasn't suggesting that you were— that you should...' She shook her head. 'It's not my place to make judgements, but——'

'Of course it is. You and your estimable father both make judgements. You judged Abu Al Zouad worthy of Bennettco's largesse, you judged Prince Khalil a man to be easily bought off——'

'Easily?' His supercilious tone made Joanna bristle and she spoke sharply, before she could stop herself. 'Who are you kidding? I know how much is waiting for him in that Swiss bank account, remember?' Her eyes narrowed. 'Wait a minute. Is that what this is all about? Are you going to try and hold us up for more?'

'And what if I did? You'd pay it. You'd pay whatever you must to get what you want.' He shot her a look so deadly she pressed back in her seat. 'That's how people like you do things. Don't waste your breath denying it!'

Joanna stared at him. What was happening here? A little while ago, he'd been all silken cordiality, and now he was treating her with an abrasive scorn that bordered on insult. He was scaring her, too, although she'd be damned if she'd ever let him know it. Well, not scaring her, exactly, that was too strong a word, but it was hard not to wish they were still seated in the civilised environs of the Oasis Restaurant.

Was that why he'd dragged her to the middle of nowhere—so he could insult her? That was certainly how it seemed. Even if he hadn't, even if he'd been deadly serious about taking her somewhere for a glass of champagne, she had absolutely no interest in it now. All she wanted was for him to turn the car around and take her back to the city, to lights and traffic and people.

'I've changed my mind about having champagne,' she said, swinging towards him. She waited for him to answer but he didn't. After a moment, she cleared her throat. 'Mr Hassan?'

'I heard you. You've changed your mind about drinking with me.'

'No, I mean, it's not that. I just—I—um—I misjudged the time earlier.' Damn! Why was she offering an explanation? 'Please turn the car around.'

'I can't do that.'

Can't? *Can't*? Joanna stared at him. 'Why not?'

'We are expected,' he said.

'You mean, you made a reservation? Well, I can't help——'

He swung to face her suddenly, and even in the shadowy interior of the car, she could see the sharp anger etched into his face.

'The sound of your voice annoys me,' he said coldly. 'Sit back, and be silent!'

Her mouth dropped open. 'What?' she said. '*What*?' She stared at him, waiting for him to say something, to apologise or offer some sort of explanation, but he didn't. 'That's it,' she snapped. 'Dammit, Mr Hassan, that's the final straw!'

'I don't like women to use vulgarities.'

'And I don't like men to behave like bullies! I'm telling you for the last time, turn this car around and take me back to Casablanca!'

He laughed in a way that made her heart leap into her throat.

'Is that a threat, Miss Bennett?'

'My father will be expecting me. If I'm not at the hotel soon——'

'How charming. Does he always wait up for your return at night?'

Her eyes flew to his face. What was that she heard in his voice? Disdain? Or was it something more?

'He'll be waiting to hear how our evening went,' she said quickly. 'And unless you want me to tell him that you——'

'Why would he do that?' He gave her a quick, terrible smile. 'Was there ever any doubt of your success?'

'Of course. There's always a chance of a slip-up when——'

'How could there have been a slip-up, once he put you in charge of dealing with the bandit Khalil?' The awful smile came again, clicking on, then off, like a light bulb. 'Surely he expected you'd get the agreement for him, one way or another.'

Joanna clasped her hands together in her lap. Something was happening here, something that was beyond her understanding. All she knew was that she didn't like it.

'If you're suggesting my father doesn't have every confidence in me,' she began, but the man beside her cut her short.

'Confidence?' The sound of his laughter was sharp. 'In what? You're no more a vice-president at Bennettco than that woman we passed in the street a while ago.'

'Of course I am!'

'What you are,' he snapped, 'is an empty-headed creature who knows nothing more important than the latest gossip!'

Colour rushed into Joanna's cheeks. 'How dare you?'

'What is the name of your secretary at Bennettco?'

'I don't have to answer your questions!'

'Do you even *have* an office there?' he demanded.

She swallowed. 'Not yet,' she said finally, 'but——'

'You are nothing,' he snarled, 'nothing! Your father insults me by sending you to me.'

'You've got this all wrong,' Joanna said quickly. 'I *am* his confidante. And his vice-president—well, I will be, when——'

'What you are,' he said grimly, 'is a Jezebel.'

She stared at him, her mouth hanging open. 'What?'

'I knew Bennett was desperate to hold on to his contract with that pig, Abu Al Zouad.' His eyes shot to her face. 'But even I never dreamed he'd offer up his daughter to get it!'

'Are you crazy? I told you, my father is ill. That's why he sent me to meet with you!'

'He sent you to do whatever had to be done to ensure success.' He threw her a look of such fury that Joanna felt herself blanch. 'If Khalil wouldn't accept one sort of bribe, surely he'd accept another.'

She felt the blood drain from her face. 'Are you saying my father... are you saying you think that I...?' She sprang towards him across the console and slammed her fist into his shoulder. 'You—you contemptible son of a bitch! I'd sooner sleep with a—a camel than——'

She cried out as the car swerved. The tyres squealed as they clawed at the verge; the brakes protested as he jammed them on, and then he swung towards her, his eyes filled with loathing.

'But it *would* be like sleeping with a camel, wouldn't it, Miss Bennett? Sleeping with a man like Khalil, I mean.'

'If you touch me,' Joanna said, trying to keep her voice from shaking, 'if you so much as put a finger on me, so help me, I'll——'

'You'll what?' His lips drew back from his teeth. 'Scream? Go right ahead, then. Scream. Scream until you can't scream any more. Who do you think will hear you?'

God. Oh, God! He was right. She looked around her wildly. There was darkness everywhere—everywhere except for his face, looming over hers, his eyes glinting with anger, his mouth hard and narrowed with scorn.

'My father,' she said hoarsely. 'My father will——'

'The scorpion of the desert is a greater worry to me than is your father.'

'Surely we can behave like civilised human beings and——?'

He laughed in her face. 'How can we, when I am the emissary of a savage?'

'I never said that!'

'No. You never did. But you surely thought it. What else would a greedy, tyrannical bandit be if not a savage?' His mouth thinned. 'But I ask you, who is the savage, Miss Bennett, the Hawk of the North—or a father who would offer his daughter to get what he wants?'

He caught her wrist as her hand flew towards his face. 'I've had enough, you—you self-centred son of a bitch! My father would no more——'

His face twisted. 'Perhaps I should have let it happen.' He leaned towards her, forcing her back in her seat. 'Maybe it wasn't your father who suggested you make this great sacrifice. Maybe it was *you* who wanted to share Khalil's bed—or did you think it would be sufficient to share mine?'

'I'd sooner die,' Joanna said, her voice rising unsteadily while she struggled uselessly to shove him off her. 'I swear, I'd sooner——'

His lips drew back from his teeth in a humourless smile. 'Just think what erotic delights a savage like me might have taught you. Enough, perhaps, to keep your useless New York friends tittering for an entire season!'

'You're disgusting! You—you make me sick to my stomach!'

His mouth dropped to hers like a stone, crushing the words on her lips. She struggled wildly, beating her free hand against his shoulder, trying to twist her face from his, but it was useless. He was all hard sinew and taut muscle that nothing would deter.

After a moment, he drew back.

'What's the matter?' he said coldly. 'Have you changed your mind about adding a little sweetening to Bennettco's bribe offer?'

Hatred darkened Joanna's eyes. 'What a fool I was to think I could deal with you in a civilised manner! You're just like your Prince, aren't you? When you can't get what you want, you just—you reach out and grab it!'

'What if I said you were wrong, Miss Bennett? What if I told you that I am not a man who takes?'

Anger made her reckless. 'I'd call you a liar,' she snapped.

To her surprise, he laughed. 'Which of us is the liar, Joanna? Or are you suggesting I not take what you are prepared to give?'

The look she gave him was pure defiance. 'I offered you nothing.'

For a long moment, their eyes held. Then he smiled, and the smile sent her heart into her throat.

'I never take that which has not been offered,' he said, very softly.

She cried out as he reached for her again but there was no way to escape him. He caught her face between his hands, holding it immobile, and bent his head to hers. She stiffened, holding her breath, preparing instinctively for the fury of his kiss, for whatever ugly show of strength and power lay ahead.

But there was no way to prepare for the reality of what happened. His lips were soft, moving against hers with slow persuasion, seeking response.

Not that it mattered. It was a useless effort. She would never, could never, respond to a man like him, a man who believed he could first terrorise a woman, then seduce her. His hands spread over her cheeks, his thumbs gliding slowly across the high arc of her cheekbones. His fingers threaded into her hair, slowly angling her head back so that his lips could descend upon hers again—and all at once, to Joanna's horror, something dark and primitive stirred deep within her soul, an excitement that made her pulse leap.

No. No, she didn't want this! But her body was quickening, her mouth was softening beneath his. Was it the way he was holding her, so that she was arched towards him, as if in supplication? Was it the heat of his body against hers?

The tip of his tongue skimmed across her mouth. She made a sound, a little moan that was barely perceptible, but he heard it. He whispered something incomprehensible against her mouth and his arms went around her and drew her close, so that her breasts were pressed against his chest.

Joanna felt the sudden erratic gallop of her heart as his mouth opened over hers. His tongue slipped between her lips, stroking against the tender flesh. Heat rose like a flame under her skin as he cupped her breast in his hand. She shuddered in his arms as his thumb moved against the hardening nipple.

'Yes,' he whispered, 'yes...'

How could this be happening? She hated him, for what he was and for the man he served—and yet, her hands were sliding up his chest, her palms were measuring the swift, sure beat of his heart as it leapt beneath her fingertips. Her head fell back; he kissed her throat and she made another soft sound that might have been surrender or despair...

He let her go with such abruptness that she fell back against the seat. Her eyes flew open; her gaze met his and they stared at each other. For an instant they seemed suspended in time, and then two circles of crimson rose in Joanna's cheeks.

Khalil smiled tightly. 'You see?' he said, almost lazily. He reached for the key and the engine roared to life. 'I never take what is not offered.'

Humiliation rose in her throat like bile. 'I get the message,' she said, fighting to keep her voice from shaking. 'I'm female, you're male, and I shouldn't have said anything to insult you or the mighty Khalil.'

'I'm happy to see you're not stupid.'

'Slow, maybe, but never stupid. Now, take me back to——'

'We are not returning to Casablanca, Joanna.'

She stared at him in disbelief. 'You can't possible think I'd still go anywhere with you after...'

Her heart rose into her throat. He *was* turning the car, but not back the way they'd come. Instead, they were jouncing across hard-packed dirt towards a long, looming shadow ahead.

'What is that?' she demanded, but the question was redundant, for in the headlights of the car she could now see what stood ahead of them.

It was a plane. A small, twin-engine plane, the same kind, she thought dizzily, as Bennettco owned. But this was not a Bennettco plane, not with that spread-winged, rapier-beaked bird painted on its fuselage.

Instinct made her cry out and swing towards him. She grabbed for the steering wheel but he caught her wrists easily with one hand and wrenched them down.

'Stop it,' he said, his voice taut with command.

The car slid to a stop. He yanked out the keys and threw the door open. Several robed figures approached, then dropped to their knees in the sand as Khalil stepped from the automobile.

'Is the plane ready for departure?' he demanded in English.

'It has been ready since we received your message, my lord,' one of the men answered without lifting his head.

Khalil hauled Joanna out after him. 'Come,' he said.

She didn't. She screamed instead, and he lifted her into his arms and strode towards the plane while her cries rose into the night with nothing but the wind to answer them. Khalil paused at the door and shoved her through. Then he climbed inside and pushed her unceremoniously into a seat.

'Let's go,' he snapped at the men scrambling up after him. 'Quickly!'

The little coterie bowed again, touching their hands to their foreheads. It was a gesture of homage that would, even moments before, have made Joanna laugh with scorn. Now, it made her dizzy with fear.

Suddenly, she understood.

'You're not the Prince's emissary,' she said, swinging towards him, 'you're—you're Khalil!'

He laughed. 'As I said, Joanna, you aren't a stupid woman.'

She leaped to her feet and spun towards his men. 'Do you understand what he's doing? He's kidnapping me! He'll lose his head for this. You'll all lose——' The plane's engines coughed to life and began to whine. Joanna turned back to Khalil. 'What do you want?' she pleaded. 'More money? You've only to ask my father. He'll give you whatever——' The plane began moving forward into the dark night and her voice rose in panic. 'Listen to me! Just take me back. No. You don't have to take me back. I can drive myself. Just give me the keys to the car and——'

Khalil's look silenced her.

'We've a three-hour flight ahead of us. I suggest you get some rest before we reach the northern hills.'

'You'll never get away with this! You can't just——'

Khalil put his hands on his hips and looked at her. His eyes were cold, empty of feeling. With a sinking heart, she thought what a fool she'd been not to have guessed his identity from the start.

'It is done,' he said. 'What will be, will be.'

Joanna stared at him, at that unyielding, harsh face, and then she turned away and looked blindly out of the porthole while the plane raced down the sand and rose into the night sky.

He was right. It was done. Now, she could only pray for deliverance.

CHAPTER FOUR

NOTHING made sense. Joanna sat stiffly in her seat, alone with her thoughts in the darkness of the plane, trying to come up with answers to questions that seemed as complex as the riddle of the Sphinx.

Why had Khalil played out the charade of letting her think he was someone else? He could have announced his identity when he'd discovered she was Joanna, not Joe.

Where was he taking her? This wasn't any quick trip around the block. She glanced at the luminescent face of her watch. They'd been in the air more than an hour now, and she'd yet to feel the tell-tale change in engine pitch and angle of flight that would mean they were readying to land. A little shudder went through her. No, she thought again, this wasn't a short hop by any means. Wherever Khalil was taking her, it was some distance from Casablanca.

And then there was the most devastating question of all, the one her frazzled brain kept avoiding.

Why had he taken her captive?

She had tiptoed around the issue half a dozen times at least, edging up to it as a doe might a clearing in the woods, getting just so close, then skittering off. She knew she had to deal with the question, and soon, for this flight could not last forever and Joanna knew herself well. Whatever lay ahead would only be the more terrifying if she weren't prepared for it mentally.

The plane bounced gently in an air pocket and she used the moment to try and see beyond the curtain that separated the tiny lounge area in which she was seated from the rest of the cabin. Khalil had gone to the front shortly after take-off, leaving her alone with a robed thug who sat in total silence. Did he speak English? She thought he must, but what was the difference? He was a brigand, the same as his chieftain, left to guard his prisoner. Where Khalil thought she might escape to was anybody's guess.

She closed her eyes. It was too late for that, too late for anything except standing up to whatever fate awaited her and showing this—this cut-throat marauder that Sam Bennett's daughter was no coward.

'Are you cold?'

Her eyes flew open. A man was standing over her, tall and fierce and incredibly masculine in flowing white robes. Joanna's throat constricted. It was Khalil.

'Are you cold, Joanna?'

'Cold?' she said foolishly, while she tried to reconcile the urbane man who'd sat beside her at dinner with this robed renegade.

'You were shivering.' His eyes, as frigid as winter ice, swept over her. 'But then you would be, wearing such a dress.' His tone oozed disdain. 'It hardly covers your body.'

Joanna felt heat flood her face. Her fingers itched with the desire to tug up the bodice of her dress, to try and tug down the emerald silk skirt, but she'd be damned if she'd give him that satisfaction. Instead, she folded her hands in her lap, her fingers laced together to keep them still, and looked straight at him.

'I am certain that Oscar de la Renta would be distressed to learn that you don't approve of his design, Your Highness, but then, the dress wasn't made for the approval of a back-country bandit.'

The insult struck home. She could see it in the swift narrowing of his eyes, but his only obvious reaction was a small, hard smile.

'I'm sure you're right, Joanna. The dress was meant for a finer purpose: to entice a man, to make him forget what he must remember and concentrate only on the female prize wrapped within it.'

Joanna smiled, too, very coldly.

'I am dressed for dinner at the Oasis. Had you told me we were going on a journey, I'd have worn something more suitable for travel.'

His smile broadened. 'Had I told you that, I somehow doubt you'd have come with me.'

It was impossible to carry off her end of the dialogue this time. He had struck too close to home, and she shuddered at the realisation.

'You *are* cold,' he said sharply. 'It is foolish to sit here and tremble when you have only to ask for a lap robe.'

It was hard to know whether to laugh or cry. A lap robe? Did he really think this was a flight on Royal Air Marroc to New York? Did he think she was wondering what would be served for dinner?

'Ahmed!' Khalil snapped his fingers and the man seated across the aisle sprang to his feet. There was a flurry of swift, incomprehensible words and then the man bowed and scurried off. 'Ahmed will find you a blanket, Joanna. If you wish anything else...'

'The only thing I want is my freedom.'

'If you wish anything else,' he said, as if she hadn't spoken, 'coffee, or perhaps tea——'

'Are you deaf or just a bastard? I said——'

She gasped as he bent and clasped her shoulders so tightly that she could feel the imprint of his fingers, the heat of his body.

'Watch your tongue! I have had enough of your mouth tonight.'

'Let go of me!'

'Perhaps you don't realise the seriousness of your situation, Joanna. Perhaps you think this is a game, that I have instructed my pilot to fly us in circles and then land at Nouasseur Airport before I return you to your hotel.'

It wasn't easy to look back at him without flinching, to force herself to meet that unyielding rock-like stare, but she did.

'What I think,' she said tightly, 'is that you've made one hell of a mistake, Khalil, and that there's still time to get out of it with your head still attached to your neck.'

He looked at her for what seemed a long time, in a silence filled only with the steady drone of the plane's engines, and then he smiled.

'How thoughtful, Joanna. Your concern for my welfare is touching.' He straightened and looked down at her. 'But you may be right. Perhaps I *have* made a mistake.'

A tiny flame of hope burst to life in her heart. 'If you take me back now,' she said quickly, 'I'll forget this ever happened.'

'Perhaps I should have accepted what you so graciously offered before I stole you.'

Joanna flew from her seat. 'How dare you say such things to me?'

'Highness?'

Khalil put his hand on her shoulders and propelled her back into her seat. He turned to Ahmed, who held a light blanket in his outstretched arms.

'Thank you, Ahmed. You may leave now.' Khalil dropped the blanket into Joanna's lap as Ahmed disappeared behind the curtain. 'Your temper should be enough to keep you warm, but if it isn't, use this.'

'Dammit!' Joanna shoved the blanket to the floor. 'Who in hell do you think you are?'

He bent, picked up the blanket, and dropped it in her lap again.

'I am the man who holds your destiny in his hands,' he said with a quick, chill smile. 'Now, cover yourself, before I do it for you.'

She snatched the blanket from him, draping it over herself so that it swathed her from throat to toe.

'What's the matter?' she said with saccharine sweetness. 'Are you afraid my father won't pay as much ransom if I come down with pneumonia and die?'

His thigh brushed hers as he sat down beside her, the softness of his robe a direct contrast to the muscled warmth of the leg beneath it.

'Such drama, Joanna. You're young and healthy and a long, long way from death.'

'But that is what you're after, isn't it?' The question she'd dreaded asking was out now, and she was glad. Still, it was hard to say the words. 'Ransom money, from my father?'

'Ransom money?' he repeated, his brows knotting together.

'Yes.' She made an impatient gesture. 'I don't know how you say it in your language—it's money paid to a kidnapper to——'

'I speak English as well as you do,' he said sharply. 'I know what the word means.'

'Well, then . . .'

'Is that what you think this is all about? Do you think me so corrupt that the money you offered me at the restaurant isn't enough to buy my co-operation?'

'What else am I to think?'

Khalil sat back, his arms folded over his chest. 'And just how much do you think you're worth?'

Joanna's jaw tightened. 'Don't play with me, Khalil. I don't like it!'

'Ah.' Amusement glinted in his eyes. 'You don't like it.'

'That's right, I don't. It's bad enough that you've kidnapped me——'

'And I don't like your choice of words.'

She stared at him in disbelief. 'What would you prefer me to call it? Shall I say that you've decided to take me on a sightseeing trip?'

His face turned cold and hard. 'What I do, I do because I must.'

Joanna sat forward, the blanket dropping unnoticed to her waist. 'All you had to do was say you wanted more money. My father would surely have been willing to——'

'Money!' His lip curled with disgust. 'You think there is a price for everything, you and your father. Well, this is what I think of your pathetic attempts to buy me!'

He dug the envelope she'd given him from his robe, folded it in half, and ripped it into pieces that floated into her lap like a paper sandstorm. For the first time, she permitted herself to admit that he might have kidnapped her for some darker, more devious reason.

'Then—then if it's not for the money...' She touched the tip of her tongue to her lips. 'I see. You want to hurt my father.'

Khalil's mouth narrowed. 'Is that what I want? It must be, if you say it is. After all, you know everything there is to know about me and my motives.'

'But you won't hurt him,' she said, leaning forward towards him. 'You'll just make him angry. And——'

'I don't give a damn what he is!' Khalil reached out quickly and caught her by the shoulders. 'He can be angry, hurt, he can slash his clothing and weep for all I care!'

'Then why—if you don't want money, if you don't care how my father takes the news of my kidn—of my abduction, what's the point? Why have you done this?'

A quick smile angled across his mouth.

'Ah, Joanna,' he said, very softly, 'I'm disappointed. You seem to know so much about the kind of man I am—surely you must have some idea.'

She stared at him, at those fathomless dark blue eyes. A tremor began deep in her muscles and she tensed her body against it, hating herself not only for her fear but for this show of weakness she must not let him see.

Before she'd left New York, the same people who'd teased her about her chances of running into the ghost of Humphrey Bogart had teased her with breathless rumours of a still-flourishing white slave trade, of harems hidden deep within the uncharted heart of the desert and the mountains that enclosed it.

'And what a prize you'd be,' a man at a charity ball had purred, 'with that pale skin, those green eyes, and all that gorgeous red hair!'

Everyone had laughed, even her—but now it didn't seem funny at all. Now, with Khalil's fingers imprinting themselves in her skin, she knew it was time to finally come face to face with the fear that had haunted her from the moment she'd found herself in this plane.

'My father won't let you get away with this,' she said in a low, taut voice.

'Your father will have no choice.'

'You underestimate him. He's a powerful man, Khalil. He'll find where you've taken me and——'

'He will know where I've taken you, Joanna. It will not be a secret.'

'He'll come after me,' she said, her voice rising, becoming just a little unsteady. 'And when he rescues me, he'll kill you!'

Khalil laughed, a soft, husky sound that made the hair rise on the nape of her neck.

'I am not so easy to kill. Abu Al Zouad will surely tell your father that.'

'How about my government? Do you think you can make a fool of it, too?'

'Your government?' His dark brows drew together. 'What part has it in this?'

She smiled piteously. 'I'm a US citizen. Perhaps, in your country, women are—are like cattle, to be bought and sold and—and disposed of at will, but in my country——'

'I know all about your country, enough to know your government won't give a damn about one headstrong woman who runs off——'

'I didn't run off! You——'

'—who runs off with a man on a romantic adventure.'

'Me, run off with you on a romantic adventure?' She laughed. 'No one would accept that! Anyway, my father will tell them the truth.'

'He'll tell them exactly what I authorise him to tell them,' Khalil said coldly.

'Don't be ridiculous! Why would he lie?'

'This thing is between your father, Abu Al Zouad, and me. No one else will be involved.'

'You're unbelievable,' Joanna said, 'absolutely unbelievable! Do you really imagine you can tell my father what to do? Maybe you should have spent more time in the West, Khalil. Maybe you'd have realised you're only

a man, not a—a tin god whose every insane wish has to
be obeyed!'

'I'm impressed,' he said, with a condescending little
smile, as if she were a pet he'd just found capable of
some clever and unexpected trick. 'Any other woman
would be begging for mercy, but not you.'

Joanna's chin lifted. 'That's right,' she said, determined not to let him see the depths of her fear, 'not me!
So if that's why you abducted me—so you could have
the pleasure of seeing me grovel and weep for mercy—
you're out of luck.'

'I'm sorry to disappoint you, Joanna, but my reasons
were hardly so petty.' He gave her a slow, lazy smile. 'I
took you because I can use you.'

Her eyes flashed to his. 'Use me?' she repeated. 'I
don't—I don't understand...'

His smile changed, took on a darkness that made her
breath catch, and his gaze moved over her lingeringly,
from her wide eyes to her parted lips, and finally to the
swift rise and fall of her breasts.

'Don't you?' he said softly.

'Khalil.' She swallowed, although the effort was almost
painful. 'Khalil, listen to me. You can't—you can't
just——'

'Shall I have you sold at the slave-market?' He took
her face in his hands and tilted it to his. 'You would
bring a king's ransom in the north, where eyes the colour
of jade and hair like the embers of a winter fire are very,
very rare.'

Oh, God, Joanna thought, oh, God...

'You wouldn't do that,' she said quickly. 'Selling me
would be——'

'It would be foolish.' He smiled again, a quick angling
of his lips that was somehow frighteningly intimate. 'For
only a fool would sell you, once he had you.'

'Abducting me is foolish, too!' She spoke quickly, desperately, determined to force him to listen to reason. 'You must know that you can't get away with——'

'What would you be like, I wonder, if I took you to my bed?'

Patches of scarlet flared in her cheeks, fury driving out the fear that had seconds before chilled her blood. 'I'd sooner die than go to your bed!'

He laughed softly. 'I don't think so, Joanna. I think you would come to it smiling.'

'Not in a million years!'

His fingers threaded into her hair; his thumbs stroked over her skin.

'How would your skin feel, against mine?' he said softly. 'Would it be hot, like fire? Or would it be cool, like moonlight against the desert sand?'

There it was again, that sense of something dark and primal stirring within her, like an unwanted whisper rising in the silence of the night.

'You'll never know,' she said quickly. 'I promise you that.'

Khalil's eyes darkened. He smiled, bent his head, brushed his lips against Joanna's. A tiny flicker of heat seemed to radiate from his mouth to hers.

'Your words are cool, but your lips are warm,' he murmured. Her breath caught as his hands slid to her midriff. She felt the light brush of his fingers just below her breasts. 'Fire and ice, Joanna. That is what you are. But I would melt that ice forever.' He pressed his mouth to her throat. 'I would turn you to hot flame that burns only for me,' he said, the words a heated whisper against her skin.

She wanted to tell him that it was he who'd burn, in the eternal fires of hell—but his arms were tightening around her, he was gathering her close, and before she could say anything he crushed her mouth under his.

He had spoken of turning her to flame but *he* was the flame, shimmering against her as he held her, his kiss branding her with heat. His tongue traced the seam of her lips, then slid against hers as her mouth opened to his, silk against silk.

Dear God, what was the matter with her? This man was everything she hated, he was her enemy, her abductor...

He felt the sudden tightening of her muscles and he reached between their bodies, caught her hands and held them fast.

'Don't fight me,' he whispered.

But she did, twisting her head away from his, panting beneath his weight. Still, he persisted, kissing her over and over until suddenly she went still and moaned his name.

'Yes,' he growled, the one word an affirmation of his triumph.

Joanna wrenched her hands from his and buried her fingers in his dark hair, drawing him down to her, giving herself up to the drowning sweetness of his kisses.

Khalil whispered something swift and fierce against her mouth. He drew her from her seat and into his lap, holding her tightly against him, his body hard beneath hers. His hand moved over her, following the curve of her hip, the thrust of her breast. Her head fell back and the dampness of wanting him bloomed like a velvet-petalled flower between her thighs. He bent and pressed his open mouth to the silk that covered her breast, and she cried out.

The sound rose between them, piercing the silence of the little cabin. Khalil drew back and Joanna did too.

They stared at each other and then, abruptly, he thrust her from him, shoving her back into her seat and rising to his feet in one swift motion.

'You see?' His eyes were like sapphire coals in his taut face; his voice was cold, tinged with barely controlled cruelty. 'I could have you now, if I wanted you. But I do not. I have never wanted any woman who offered her body in trade.'

Joanna sprang towards him, sputtering with fury, her hand upraised, but Khalil caught her wrist and twisted her arm behind her.

'I warn you,' he said through his teeth, 'you are done insulting me, you and your father both!'

'Whatever it is you're planning, Khalil, I promise you, you won't get away with it.'

He looked at her for a long moment, still holding her close to him, and then he laughed softly.

'It's dangerous to threaten me, Joanna. Surely you've learned that much by now.'

His gaze fell to her mouth. She tensed, waiting for him to gather her to him and kiss her again. This time, she was prepared to claw his face if she had to rather than let him draw her down into that silken darkness— but suddenly a voice called out from beyond the curtain.

Khalil's smile faded. 'We have arrived.'

She fell back as he let go of her. 'Where?' she asked, but he was already hurrying up the aisle towards the front of the plane.

She knelt in her seat and leaned towards the window. Some time during their confrontation, the plane had not only descended, it had landed. She pressed her nose to the glass. It was still night, yet she could see very clearly, thanks to a full moon and what at first seemed the light from at least a hundred lamps.

Her breath caught. Torches! Those were flaming torches, held aloft by a crowd of cheering men mounted on horseback.

With a little moan, she put her hands to her mouth and collapsed back into her seat.

They had arrived, all right—they'd arrived smack in the middle of the thirteenth century!

CHAPTER FIVE

IT WAS the sight of the horsemen that changed everything. Until now, Joanna had let herself half believe that if what was happening was not a dream, it was some sort of terrible prank, one that would end with the plane turning and heading back to Morocco.

But the line of horses standing just outside the plane, the robed men on their backs, the torches casting a glow as bright as daylight over the flat plateau on which they'd landed, finally forced her to acknowledge the truth.

Khalil had stolen her away from the world she knew. What happened to her next was not in the hands of fate but in the hands of this man, this bandit—and he didn't give a damn for the laws of his country or of civilisation.

'Joanna.'

She looked up. He was standing at the open door of the plane, his face like granite.

'Come,' he said.

Come. As if she were a slave, or a dog. Joanna's jaw clenched. That was what he wanted, to reduce her to some sub-human status, to stress his domination over her and make her cower beneath it. In some ways, he'd already succeeded. She had let him see her fear when he'd first abducted her, let him see it again when she'd pleaded with him to release her.

She drew a deep, deep breath. And her fear had been painfully obvious when he'd kissed her and she'd yielded herself so shamelessly in his arms. It was nothing but fear that had caused her to react to him that way. She knew it, and he did, too.

But his ugly scheme could only work if she let it—and she would not. She would never, ever let him see her fear again.

'Joanna!' Her head came up. He was waiting for her, his hands on his hips, his legs apart, looking as fierce as the predatory bird whose name he bore. 'Are you waiting for me to come and get you?'

She rose, head high, spine straight. He didn't move as she made her way slowly towards him, but she saw his gaze sweep over her, his eyes narrowing, his jaw tightening, and she knew he must be once again telling himself that only a woman who wanted to seduce a man would dress in such a way.

It was laughable, really. Her dress was fashionable and expensive, but it was basically modest and would not have raised an eyebrow anywhere but here or the Vatican. For a second, she wished she'd gone with her first instinct and worn a business suit, but then she thought no, let him have to look at her for the next hours—which was surely only as long as he would keep her here—let him look at her and be reminded constantly that she was of the West, that he could not treat her as he would one of his women, that she was Sam Bennett's daughter and he'd damned well better not forget it.

'You are not dressed properly.'

Joanna smiled coolly. He was as transparent as glass.

'I am dressed quite properly.' She gave him an assessing look, taking in the long, white robe he wore, and then she smiled again. 'It is you who are not dressed properly. Men stopped wearing skirts a long time ago.'

To her surprise, he laughed. 'Try telling that to some of my kinsmen.' With a swift movement, he shrugged off his white robe. Beneath it, he wore a white tunic and pale grey, clinging trousers tucked into high leather boots. 'You are not dressed for these mountains.' Briskly, as if she were a package that needed wrapping, Khalil dropped the robe over her shoulders and enfolded her in it. 'We have a climate like that of the desert. By day, it is warm—but when the sun drops from the sky the air turns cold.'

She wanted to protest, to tell him she didn't need anything from him, but it was too late. He had already drawn the robe snugly around her and anyway, he was right. There was a bone-numbing chill drifting in through the open door. Joanna drew the robe more closely around her. It was still warm from Khalil's body and held a faint, clean scent that she knew must be his. A tremor went through her again, although there was no reason for it.

'Thank you,' she said politely. 'Your concern for my welfare is touching. I'll be sure and mention it to my father so he'll know that my abductor was a gentle—hey! What are you doing? Put me down, dammit! I'm perfectly capable of walking.'

'In those shoes?' He laughed as he lifted her into his arms. 'It was the ancient Chinese who kept their women in servitude by making it impossible for them to walk very far, Joanna. My people expect their women to stride as well as a man.' He grinned down at her. 'If you were to sprain your ankle, how would you tend the goats and chickens tomorrow?'

Goats? Chickens? Was he serious?

'I won't be here tomorrow,' she said curtly.

'You will be here as long as I want you here,' he said, and stepped from the plane.

A full-throated cheer went up from Khalil's assembled warriors when they saw him. They edged their horses forward, their flaming torches held high. He stood still for a moment, smiling and accepting their welcome, and then one of the men looked at her and said something that made the others laugh. Khalil laughed, too, and then he began to speak.

Joanna knew he must be talking about her. His arms tightened around her and he held her out just a little, as if she were a display. The faces of his men snapped towards her and a few of them chuckled.

'Damn you,' she hissed, 'what are you saying about me?'

Khalil looked down at her. 'Hammad asked why I'd brought home such a lumpy package.' His teeth flashed in a quick grin. 'I suggested he remember the old saying about never judging a horse by the saddle blanket that covers it.'

Her face pinkened. 'It's a book one isn't supposed to judge in my country,' she said frigidly. 'And I would remind you that I am neither.'

His smile fled, and his face took on that stony determination she'd already come to know too well.

'No,' he said grimly, 'you are not. What you are is a guarantee that I will get what I want from Sam Bennett.'

So. It was ransom he wanted, after all. Despite all his cryptic word-games, it was money he would trade her for.

One of his men moved forward, leading a huge black stallion that tossed its head and whickered softly. Khalil lifted Joanna on to its back, then mounted behind her. She stiffened as his arms went around her.

'Yet another indignity you must suffer,' he said, his voice low, his breath warm against her ear as he gathered the reins into his hands. 'But only for a little while, Joanna. Soon, we will be at my home, and neither of us will have to tolerate the sight and touch of the other until morning.'

He murmured something to the horse. It pricked its ears and it began moving forward, its steps high and almost delicate. Khalil spoke again, and the animal began moving faster, until it seemed to be racing across the plateau with the wind. Khalil's arms tightened around her; there was no choice but to lean back and let his hard body support hers as they galloped into the night.

How long would it take to get his ransom demand to her father? And how long after that for the money to reach here?

Khalil's arm brushed lightly, impersonally, across her breast as he urged the horse on.

Not too long, she thought. Please, let it not take too long.

It couldn't possibly.

Her father would want her back, and quickly, no matter how outrageous the Prince's demands.

She had assumed the torchlight greeting had been ceremonial. It had been handsome, she'd thought grudgingly, even impressive, but a man who owned a private plane would not also be a man who travelled his country on the back of a horse.

But an hour or more of riding had changed Joanna's mind. There was nothing ceremonial about riding a horse in terrain such as this, she thought, wincing a little as she shifted her bottom and tried to find a spot that hadn't already become sensitised to the jouncing and bouncing of the saddle. The plane had landed on a plateau, but from what she'd seen so far that had probably been the only flat space in a hundred miles.

Ever since, they'd been climbing into the mountains, although calling these massive, rocky outcroppings 'mountains' was like calling the horse beneath her a pony. The resemblance was purely accidental. The moon had risen, casting a pale ivory light over the landscape, tipping the tall pines that clung to the steep slopes with silver.

How far up would they ride? It was probable that a bandit would want to have a hidden stronghold, but this was ridiculous! Only a mountain goat could possibly clamber up this high.

Suppose her father and the Sultan mounted a rescue mission? Could they make it? No. It was best not to think that way. She had to think positively, had to concentrate on how easily they'd find her. And they would. Of course they would. Khalil wasn't invincible and his hideout, no matter how it resembled the eyrie of a hawk, would not be impregnable.

Her father would come for her. He would find her. He would take her back to civilisation, and all this would just be a dream.

A dream. Joanna yawned. She was tired. Exhausted, really, and the slow, steady gait of the horse, the creak of leather, the jingle of the tiny bells that adorned the bridle, were all having a hypnotic effect. She yawned again, then blinked hard, trying to keep her eyes open. It would be so nice to rest for a few minutes.

Her head fell back, her cheek brushed lightly against a hard, warm surface. Quickly, she jerked upright.

'Joanna?'

'Yes?'

'Are you tired?'

'No. I'm not.'

'You must be.' Khalil lifted his hand to her cheek. 'Put your head against my shoulder, and sleep for a while.'

'Don't be ridiculous! I'd sooner——'

'Sleep with a camel. Yes, I know.' He laughed. 'Just pretend that's what I am, then, and put your head back and close your eyes.'

'Please,' she said coldly, 'spare me this attempt at solicitude. It doesn't become you.'

Khalil sighed. 'As you wish, Joanna.'

The horse plodded on, its movements slow and steady. Up, down, up, down...

Concentrate. Concentrate. Listen to the sounds, to the clatter of the horse's hooves, to the sigh of the wind through the trees.

Stay awake! Take deep breaths. Smell the fragrance of pine carried on the night wind, the scent of leather and horse...

'Dammit, woman, you're as stubborn as the wild horses of Chamoulya! Stop being such a little fool and get some rest.'

'I don't need rest. I don't need anything. And I especially don't need your help.'

'Fine. I'll remember that.' He jerked her head back against his shoulder. 'Now, shut up and stop fidgeting. You're making Najib nervous, and——'

'Najib?'

'My horse. And the last thing I want is for Najib to be nervous on the climb ahead.'

Najib, she thought giddily. She was making Najib nervous. By heaven, this man was crazy! He had kidnapped her, carried her off to God only knew where without so much as giving a damn if she turned to stone with fright, but he was worried that she was making his horse nervous.

Joanna's eyes flickered shut. Still, he was right. It would be stupid to upset the animal on a narrow mountain path. Closing her eyes didn't mean she'd sleep. She'd let her other senses take over. Yes. That was what she'd do, she'd—she'd think about the coolness of the night air—and the contrasting warmth of Khalil's arms, think about the softness of his robe on her skin and the contrasting hardness of his thighs, cradling her hips.

That was the word that best described him. He was hard. Powerful. That was how he felt, holding her—and yet she knew his hands were holding the reins lightly. Still, the black stallion responded readily to his slightest touch, to the press of his heel.

A woman would respond to him that way, too, Joanna thought drowsily; she would move eagerly to obey him, to pleasure him and to let him pleasure her...

A heat so intense it was frightening spread through her body. Her eyes flew open and she jerked upright in the saddle, steadying herself by clasping the pommel. Najib snorted and tossed his head, and Khalil caught her and pulled her back against him.

'Dammit!' he said tightly. 'What did I tell you about making the horse nervous?'

'I know what you said,' Joanna snapped, 'and frankly, I don't much care if I make your horse nervous or...'

A whimper slipped from her throat as she looked down. They were on a ledge that looked only slightly wider than a man's hand. Below, the earth dropped away, spinning into darkness.

'Exactly,' Khalil said gruffly.

Joanna didn't have to ask him what he meant. She turned her face away from the precipice.

'The stallion is sure-footed, Joanna. But I would prefer he have no distractions.'

She laughed uneasily. 'That's—that's fine with me. Tell him—tell him to pay no attention to me, please. No attention at all.'

Khalil laughed softly. 'I'll tell him. Now, why don't you shut your eyes again and sleep?'

'I wasn't sleeping,' she said. 'How could anyone sleep, on the back of this—this creature?'

'I'm sure it's a sacrifice when you're accustomed to riding in the back of a chauffeured limousine.'

She smiled smugly. 'No greater than the sacrifice one makes giving up the comfort of a private plane for the back of a horse.'

'The plane is necessary,' he said, so quickly that she knew she'd stung him. 'My responsibilities take me in many different directions.'

'Oh, I'm sure they do.' Her voice was like honey. 'They take you up mountains and down mountains—clearly, one needs a plane for that!'

He said nothing, but she had the satisfaction of seeing his jaw tighten. They rode on in silence while the moon dropped lower in the sky, and then, finally, Khalil lifted his hand and pointed into the distance.

'There it is,' he said quietly. 'Bab al Sama—Gate to the Sky. My home.'

Joanna sat up straighter and stared into the darkness. There were smudges against the horizon. What were they?

'Tents,' Khalil said, as if she'd asked the question aloud. 'Some of my people still cling to the old ways.'

Tents. Of course. His people lived outside the law. They'd want to be able to strike camp quickly.

But the tents were larger than she'd expected. They were, in fact, enormous. And what was that beyond them? Joanna caught her breath. It was a walled city, ancient and serene in the moonlight. A gateway loomed ahead and the horsemen filed through it, then stopped inside the courtyard of a stone building. The cluster of men dismounted, as did Khalil, and then he looked up at Joanna and lifted his arms to her.

'Come.'

Come. Joanna's chin lifted. There it was again, that single, imperious command. She tossed her head, delib-

erately turned away from him, and threw her leg over
the saddle.

'Joanna!' Khalil's angry voice stopped her for an instant. He moved quickly, so that despite her efforts to
avoid him she slid into his arms. 'You little fool! Didn't
anyone ever teach you there's a right way and a wrong
way to mount a horse?'

'I wasn't mounting him, I was getting off!' She put
her hands on his shoulders. 'Put me down!'

'Horses are skittish creatures, Joanna. Surely, even
you know that.' His eyes glared into hers. 'They're
trained to accept a rider from the left side—but anyone
coming at them from the right is asking for trouble.'

'I'll be sure and remember the next time,' she said
with heavy sarcasm. 'Now, put me down!'

'With pleasure.' She gasped as he dropped her to her
feet. 'Goodnight, Joanna. I suggest you get some rest.
You've a long day ahead of you.'

She watched in disbelief as he turned on his heel and
marched away from her.

'Goodnight?' she said. Her voice rose. 'What do you
mean, goodnight? Where am I supposed to sleep, Khalil?
Out here, with the horses?'

He spun towards her, and she saw the quick, humourless flash of his teeth.

'I think too much of them to subject them to an entire
night in your company.'

'Damn you, Khalil! You can't just...'

'*Mademoiselle*?'

Joanna turned quickly. A girl had come up silently
behind her. She was slender, with long, dark hair and
wide-set eyes.

'I am Rachelle, *mademoiselle*. I am to see to
your comfort.'

Joanna's mouth narrowed as she looked at the girl. 'I suppose you usually see to the Prince's comfort.'

Rachelle's smooth brow furrowed. '*Mademoiselle*?'

Joanna sighed. It wasn't this child's fault that she had to play slave to a rogue. She forced a faint, weary smile to her lips.

'I could use some comfort. A basin of warm water, a cup of hot tea, and a soft, comfortable bed would be lovely.'

The girl smiled. 'It will be my pleasure, *mademoiselle*. If you will please follow me...?'

Warm water, tea, a comfortable bed—in the mountain hideaway of Khalil the bandit Prince? It was all out of the question and Joanna knew it, but she was too tired to care. A wash in a mountain stream, a cup of cold water, and a blanket spread on the floor were the best she could hope for, but after the last few hours even they would be welcome.

And tomorrow—tomorrow, her father would come for her. He wouldn't wait for Khalil's ransom demand. She was certain of it. Why would he waste time, and risk her life? By now, he would know that she was missing, and it wouldn't take any great effort to know what had happened to her. As for locating her—her father's resources were endless, his contacts enormous. He'd find her, and come after her, before the next setting of the sun.

Joanna's shoulders went back as she marched into the stone building on Rachelle's heels.

'You're the one who's going to need a good night's sleep, Your Highness,' she muttered. 'Because as of tomorrow, you're going to find yourself neck-deep in trouble!'

'*Mademoiselle*? Did you say something?'

Joanna cleared her throat. 'I said, I think I'd like a sandwich to go with that tea, Rachelle. Can you manage that, do you think?'

The girl stopped and turned to face her. 'Certainly. My lord has made it clear that I am to do whatever pleases you, *mademoiselle*. You have only to tell me, and I will obey.'

Joanna gave her a bright, beaming smile. 'How about giving me a map and a ticket out of here?'

Rachelle smiled uncertainly. 'I do not understand...'

'You know, point me towards the nearest highway and send me on my way.'

'*Mademoiselle* jokes,' the girl said, with another little smile.

Joanna sighed. '*Mademoiselle* is dead serious. The only thing I really want is to get away from your lord and master.'

Rachelle ducked her head, as if Joanna's words had unsettled her. 'Here is your room,' she said, and opened the nearest door.

Joanna stepped inside the room. It was dimly lit, and what little light there was fell across a huge bed. An image flashed into her mind. She saw herself on that bed, locked in Khalil's arms, her mouth open to his, her breasts tightening under the slow, sweet stroke of his fingers...

'Stop it,' she hissed.

The girl looked at her. '*Mademoiselle*?'

Joanna puffed out her breath. She *did* need a night's rest. Hallucinations weren't her style, but she'd surely just had one. Any second now, a chorus line of pink elephants would probably come tap-dancing into view!

'I—uh—I think I'll pass on the tea and all the rest, Rachelle.' Joanna sank down wearily on the edge of the bed. 'Just turn out the lights and hang out the "do not disturb" sign.'

'I am afraid I do not understand...'

Joanna sighed. 'I just want to get to bed. It's very late, and I'm exhausted.'

'As you wish, *mademoiselle*.'

Sleep, Joanna thought as the girl moved silently around the room, sleep was precisely what she needed. It would clear her head, drive away the cobwebs. And, when she awoke, her father would probably be here, ready to take her home and make the almighty Khalil eat his every threatening, insolent word.

And that, she thought with grim satisfaction, would almost be enough to make this horrible night worthwhile.

CHAPTER SIX

JOANNA lay asleep in her bed, dreaming... Her father and a rotund little man sat in a pool of light, their heads bent over what looked like a game board while she sat in the darkened perimeter of the room, watching, when the silence was broken by the sound of hoofbeats. She looked up just in time to see a man on the back of a great ebony stallion bearing down on her.

Father, she cried. She wanted to run, but her legs wouldn't move. *Father*, she said again as the horseman leaned down, snatched her up, and tossed her across his saddle.

But her father didn't hear. He was intent on his opponent and on moving his playing piece around the board, and even though she called and called him he didn't——

'Good morning, *mademoiselle*.'

Joanna awoke instantly, her heart racing. The room was unfamiliar, grey and shadowed, and she stared blindly at the figure silhouetted against the drawn window curtains.

'Khalil?' she said shakily.

'It is Rachelle, *mademoiselle*.' The curtains whisked open and Joanna blinked in the golden sunlight that splashed across the bed.

'Rachelle.' Joanna expelled her breath. 'I—I was dreaming...' She sat up, her knees tenting the blanket, and pushed her hair back from her face. 'What time is it? It feels late.'

The serving girl smiled as she placed a small inlaid tray on the low table beside the bed.

'It is mid-morning, *mademoiselle*. I have brought you coffee and fruit.'

'Mid-morning? But I never sleep so...'

'My lord said to let you sleep.'

'Did he,' Joanna said, her voice flat.

The girl nodded. 'He said there was no reason to awaken you until he was ready to see you.'

Joanna snorted. 'That arrogant ass!'

Rachelle threw her a shocked look. 'We do not speak of our Prince that way, *mademoiselle*.'

'No? Well, maybe you should. Maybe you should start seeing him for the miserable donkey's *derrière* he really is!'

Rachelle's eyes widened. 'Please, *mademoiselle*. You must not say such things!'

Joanna sighed. What was the sense in taking out her frustration on a servant? The girl had no choice but to serve her master; hearing unkind things said about him clearly made her nervous. Perhaps she was afraid she'd be punished for permitting Joanna to make such remarks—the Jandaran version of guilt by association. It was the sort of thing that went on in dictatorships, wasn't it?

'Sorry,' Joanna said, with a little smile. 'I'm just feeling out of sorts this morning.'

Rachelle nodded. 'A bath will make you feel better. I have already run it. I added bath oil. I hope the scent is to your liking, *mademoiselle*. Is there something else I can get you?'

Yes, Joanna thought, you can get me my freedom. But she knew it was pointless to ask. The girl was obviously scared to death of Khalil, and desperate to avoid confrontation.

'No,' she said, after a moment, 'no, thanks. I can't think of anything more.'

'I will bring you some yogurt, *mademoiselle*, when you are finished bathing. Or would you prefer eggs?'

'I would prefer you call me Joanna. It makes me uncomfortable to have you address me so formally.'

Rachelle blushed. 'I am honoured.'

'For goodness' sake, you needn't be ''honoured''! This is the millennium. Bowing and scraping went out with the Dark Ages.'

'Yes, Joanna.' Rachelle smiled sweetly. 'If you need me, you have only to ring the bell.'

She started towards the door, and suddenly Joanna's good intentions deserted her. She couldn't let the girl leave without at least trying to get through to her.

'Rachelle!' Joanna swung her legs to the floor. 'Rachelle, wait a minute.' The girl turned towards her. 'Prince Khalil brought me here against my will,' she said in a rush. 'He kidnapped me...'

Rachelle's eyes grew shuttered. 'I shall return,' she said, and the door swung shut after her.

Joanna sat staring at it for a long moment and then she muttered several short, impolite words she'd learned during the years she'd spent with Sam in his field operations and had never found suitable to use—until now. She sat up, threw back the blankets, and looked around the room.

It was handsome, she thought grudgingly. The tiled floor, the inlaid furniture, and the white walls on which hung old and beautiful Persian rugs were all pleasing to the eye.

But it was still a prison.

She rose from the bed, kicked aside her shoes, stubbing her toe in the process, and strode briskly to the adjoining bathroom. By now, she knew better than to expect to find a hole in the ground and a basin of cold water, but the tiled room and glass-enclosed shower still were enough to surprise her. Steam rose from a deep tub, and the scent of roses filled the air.

'His Almighty Highness likes to live well,' Joanna muttered as she yanked her slip over her head and tossed it on to the closed bathroom commode.

She glared at the tub, then turned her back on it, pulled open the door to the shower stall, and stepped inside. Khalil had given orders she was not to be disturbed this morning. Had he also given orders she was to be wooed with a scented bath? A shower, quick and modern, was more to her liking.

What insanity this was. First there'd been those silly men last night, riding up to greet Khalil with torches blazing in their hands, looking like nothing so much as a crowd of extras who'd wandered off a movie set, and now there was this silly girl, Rachelle, acting as if she either lived in mortal terror of offending her lord and master—or had been brainwashed to think of him as a tin god. Either way, it was ridiculous.

'Ridiculous,' Joanna said sharply, and she shut off the spray and stepped out on to the bath mat.

She dried off briskly, reached for her slip—and stopped. She'd slept in it last night rather than have to ring for Rachelle and ask for a nightgown or pyjamas. Now, the thought of putting on the wrinkled garment was not appealing. The thought of getting into the bit of emerald silk that lay on a chair in the bedroom wasn't appealing, either, but what choice did she have? Joanna's nostrils flared. Khalil hadn't exactly given her time to pack an overnight bag!

Well, she thought, wrapping the towel around herself, she could avoid wearing the slip, at least. The dress didn't really require more than panties and a bra, both of which...

She cried out as she stepped into the bedroom. A man was standing looking out of the window, his back to the room, but she knew instantly it was Khalil. No one else would have those broad shoulders, that tapered waist, those long, muscular legs. Yes, it was certainly Khalil, making himself at home.

'What do you think you're doing?' she demanded.

Khalil turned slowly and looked at her. Rachelle had said she'd drawn a bath for the woman. Why hadn't it occurred to him that he might well catch her as she emerged from that bath, looking scrubbed and innocent and beautiful when she was none of those things? No. He was wrong. She *was* beautiful, more beautiful now, without her make-up and jewellery, than she'd been last night.

He felt a tightening in his groin and it infuriated him. That he should be stirred by a woman like this was impossible. Despite her beauty, she was hardly a prize, not when she was nothing but the *baksheesh* meant to corrupt him.

'I asked you a question! What are you doing in my room?'

His dark brows rose a little. 'Rachelle told me you were awake, and so——'

'And so you thought you'd barge right in, without permission?'

'I knocked, several times, but you didn't answer.'

'I was in the shower!'

'Yes.' He leaned back against the wall and let his gaze drift over her. 'So I see.'

Joanna flushed. She felt as if he'd stripped away the towel and she was certain that was just the way he wanted her to feel. She ached to race back to the safety of the bathroom or to drag the blanket from the bed and enclose herself in it, but she'd be damned if she'd give him the satisfaction.

'Perhaps you can also see that I wasn't exactly expecting to receive visitors,' she said coldly.

'Rachelle said you were unhappy with her.'

'So?'

'So, she is very young, and very sensitive. And——'

'Let me get this straight. You came barging into my room because I hurt Rachelle's feelings?' Joanna laughed. 'You'll forgive me, Your Lordship——'

'That is not my title.'

'If you're waiting for me to apologise for upsetting your little slave, you're in for a long wait.'

'She is not my slave.' Khalil's eyes turned cool. 'We have no slaves, here in the northern hills.'

'Of course,' Joanna purred. 'I should have realised. The people here are all happy and content. The only slaves in Jandara are in the south, where the evil Abu Al Zouad rules.'

His eyes narrowed. The woman was impossible! How dared she speak to him with so little respect? How dared she stand before him as she did, flaunting her almost naked body?

'Don't you have a robe to put on?' he demanded.

She smiled sweetly. 'I'm afraid the hotel didn't supply one.'

'Rachelle was told to bring you anything you requested. If you had thought to ask——'

'The only thing I thought to ask for was my freedom,' Joanna said, lifting her chin in defiance. 'It was a request your little harem girl denied.'

'I shall see to it that you are given some proper clothing,' Khalil said stiffly.

'Meaning what? If you think I'm going to put on a robe that drapes me from chin to toe, if you think I'm going to wrap a scarf around my head and look out at the world through a veil——'

'Is that what you have seen Rachelle wearing?'

It wasn't, of course. The girl wore a soft, scoop-necked cotton blouse and a pretty skirt that fell to mid-calf; her hair hung loose and uncovered to her shoulders.

'Or is that description of your own invention, meant to shore up your belief that we are a backward people?' The flush that rose in her cheeks gave him a certain grim satisfaction. He shrugged his white robe from his shoulders and held it out to her. 'Here. Wear this until——'

'I don't want anything from you, Khalil!'

His mouth thinned. 'Put it on!'

Her eyes flashed as he stepped forward and draped the robe over her shoulders. His fingers brushed her bare skin; a tingle raced along her nerve endings, one that sent a tremor through her. Khalil frowned and stepped back quickly.

'I will see to the clothing.'

'Yes. So you said.' Joanna drew the robe around herself. 'But I'm more interested in what my father's had to say.'

His frown deepened. 'What do you mean?'

'Come on, Khalil, don't treat me like a fool! Surely you've contacted him with your ransom demands.'

He looked at her for a long moment, then turned and strolled to the window.

'I have, yes,' he said, his back to her.

'And?' Joanna took a step forward. 'What did he say? How soon will he meet them?'

'I cannot tell you that.'

'What do you mean, you can't tell me?' Joanna moved closer to him. 'I've every right to know how long I'm going to be your prisoner!'

He swung towards her, his face stony. 'You will be here until your father decides to be reasonable.'

'You mean, I'll be here until he can raise the money you've asked for my return!'

'I have not asked for money.'

'No.' Joanna's smile was chill. 'Of course you haven't. I keep forgetting—you're the Hawk of the North. It's Abu Al Zouad who's the villain in this piece.'

'Joke all you wish, Joanna. It will not change the truth.'

Her chin lifted. 'It certainly won't. Abu Al Zouad's supposed to be this—this monster, this evil emperor, but——'

'He is a man who has enslaved his people.'

'Don't be ridiculous! If there were slaves in Jandara, Bennettco wouldn't have——'

'There are all kinds of slavery,' Khalil said sharply. 'People who live in fear of displeasing their ruler may not be slaves in the classic sense, but they are slaves just the same.'

Joanna smiled coolly. 'I suppose *your* people do that ridiculous bowing to you out of love, not fear.'

It pleased her to see a wash of crimson rise across his high cheekbones.

'It is custom,' he said sternly, 'and foolish. I have tried to change it——'

'Yeah.' She laughed. 'I'll bet.'

'My people obey me out of respect. If they thought I was wrong, the elders would say so.'

'Remarkable! You've got yourself believing your own lies!'

'And what, precisely, is that supposed to mean?' he said, glaring at her.

'You know damned well what it means! You make yourself out to be this benevolent ruler, this wonderful good guy, but you're not! You're—you're——'

'A thief. A despot. A greedy pig who wants whatever he can get from Bennettco, or else I'll——' His brow furrowed. 'I never did ask, Joanna, what is it, exactly, that I'll do to the operation if I'm not properly bought off?'

'How should I know?' she cried angrily. 'Raid the camp. Harass the workers. Disrupt things any way you can. Does it matter?'

'And if I told you that you're wrong...?'

'Listen, Khalil, I'm not going to play this silly game! You want to pretend you're Lawrence of Arabia? Fine. Wear that foolish outfit. Ride that ridiculous horse. Stand around and look fierce while your people prostrate themselves before you. As for me, all I want——'

She cried out as he caught hold of her shoulders.

'All you want,' he said through his teeth, 'is to categorise me. And if I don't fit, you'll poke, prod, shove and squeeze until I do!'

'All I want,' Joanna said, her eyes snapping defiance, 'is to go back to Casablanca.'

'Nothing would suit me better! A scorpion would make a better guest than you!'

'I am not your guest!'

'Indeed you are not.' His lip curled with distaste. 'You are an unwelcome visitor.'

'Fine! Then put me on your plane and send me back!'

'I shall, the instant your father agrees to my conditions.'

'Well, then,' she said, tossing her head, 'tell your pilot to rev up those engines. Your money should be on its way.'

A furrow appeared between his dark eyebrows. 'Your father has yet to answer me, Joanna.'

She stared at him. 'I don't understand.'

'It is quite simple. He knows what I want for your return, but he has not offered a reply.'

Joanna's eyes searched his face. 'You mean, your messenger didn't wait for one.'

Khalil shook his head. 'I mean what I said.' His words were clipped and cold. 'Your father has not responded.'

'Well, how could he? If you asked some unholy sum of money, a million billion dollars or whatever, he'd have to find a way to——'

He gave her a thin smile. 'Is that what you think you're worth?'

'The question isn't what *I* think I'm worth,' she said coldly. 'It's what *you* think you can get for me.'

'I have asked a great deal,' he said, his eyes on her face.

Why did his answer make her heartbeat quicken? The words were simple, yet they seemed to hold a complexity of meaning. Joanna gave him what she hoped was an easygoing smile.

'Really.'

'A great, great deal,' he said softly.

'All right, tell me. How many dollars am I worth?'

'I didn't ask for dollars.'

'Swiss francs, then. Or Deutschmarks. Or——'

'I told you before, I want no money for you.'

Joanna's attempted nonchalance vanished. 'For God's sake,' she snapped, 'what did you ask from my father, then? Diamonds? Gold?'

Khalil's eyes met hers. 'I have demanded that your father withdraw from the contract with Abu Al Zouad.'

'What?'

'I said——'

'I heard you—but I don't believe you. All this talk about how you love your people and how they love you, and now you're trying to blackmail Bennettco into pulling out of a million-dollar deal that would pump money and jobs into your country?'

Khalil's eyes darkened. 'He is to withdraw from it and restructure it, so that the people benefit, not Abu.'

'Oh. Oh, of course. You want him to rewrite the contract——'

'Exactly.'

'—to rewrite it according to your dictates.'

'Yes.'

Joanna laughed. 'You're good at this, you know that? I mean, if I didn't know better, I'd almost believe you! Come on, Khalil. The only benefit you have in mind is for yourself.'

His expression hardened. 'Think what you will, Joanna. I have sent your father the terms of your release. Now, it is up to him to reply.'

'He will. He definitely will. And when he does——'

But Sam should have replied already, she thought with a start. He should have said, OK, I'll do whatever you want, just set my daughter free.

No. No, he couldn't do that. She wasn't looking at things clearly. Sam wasn't about to cave in, not without being certain Khalil would live up to his end of the deal. Kidnappers were not known for honouring their agreements; her father would want to do everything in his power to satisfy himself that he could trust Khalil to let her go before he said yes, otherwise he might put her in even greater jeopardy.

She looked up. Khalil was watching her closely. His expression was unreadable, but the little smile of triumph that had been on his lips moments ago was gone. In its place was a look that might almost have been sympathy.

'I cannot imagine your father will have trouble deciding which he prefers,' he said softly, 'his daughter or his contract with the sultan.'

Joanna flushed. The bastard wasn't feeling sympathy, he was just worried that her father might not give him what he'd asked for!

'My father's an astute businessman,' she said. 'Why should he trust you? He'll want some guarantee that you won't hurt me after he agrees to your demands.'

'My message made no mention of hurting you,' he said stiffly.

'Ah. I see. You simply told him you'd keep me as your guest forever if he didn't do what you wanted.'

Khalil began to grin. 'Something like that.'

Joanna's jaunty smile faded. 'What do you mean?'

He shrugged lazily. 'I suggested that if he did not want you back, we would accommodate you here.'

'Accommodate me?'

'You would learn to live among my people.' Still smiling, he strolled across the room to where her green silk dress lay across the chair. 'It will not be the life you know,' he said, picking up the dress. It slipped through his fingers, incongruously delicate and insubstantial, and fell back to the chair. 'But at least it would stop your complaining.'

'What are you talking about?'

'Our women lead busy lives. Only idle women have time to complain. You would start simply, tending the chickens and the goats, but if you showed you were interested in learning they would teach you to cook, to spin——'

'Never!' The word exploded from her lips. 'Never, do you hear me? I'd sooner—I'd sooner——'

'What would you sooner do?' He looked across the room at her, his eyes dark. 'Surely, you would have to do something. We are all productive here, everyone but the sick, the elderly, and the children.'

He started slowly towards her. Joanna's heart skipped a beat. She wanted to step back, to put as much distance as the confines of the room permitted between herself and the man pacing towards her, but she was determined to stand her ground.

'You fit none of those categories,' he said, stopping inches from her. He gave her a long, slow look, one that left a trail of heat across her skin and she thought suddenly that it was a good thing she hadn't fought him about giving her his robe, for if she had—if she had, he would surely see the quickening of her breath, the flush that she felt rising over her entire body, the terrible, hateful way her breasts were lifting and hardening as he looked at her.

'You are not elderly, or ill, or a child, Joanna,' he said softly. He reached his hand out to her and caught a strand of auburn hair between his fingers. 'I would have to find some other use for you, I'm afraid.'

'My father will come for me,' she said fiercely. 'And—and when he does——' Her breath caught as he put his arms around her.

'I think,' he said, his voice husky, 'I think I would not waste you on the goats, even if you wished it.'

'I would rather——' He put his lips to her hair and she swallowed hard. 'I would rather tend the goats than—than——'

'One of the laws we live by is that every person should do what he or she is best suited for.' He lowered his head and nuzzled the robe from the juncture of shoulder and throat. His mouth moved lightly against her skin. 'And you,' he said, his voice dropping to a whisper, 'you are surely best suited to be with a man, to sigh his name, and drive him to the point where his bones begin to melt.'

His teeth closed lightly on her flesh. Joanna gasped, and he touched his tongue to the pinpoint of pain, soothing it away.

'You smell of flowers,' he whispered, 'of flowers heated by the sun of the desert.'

Trembling, Joanna fought for control. 'I—I smell of soap,' she said as he pressed kisses across her shoulder. 'I—I didn't use Rachelle's precious bath oils to——'

'Then the scent in my nostrils is of you.' He threaded his hand into her hair, knotting it around his fist like a bright, gleaming band, so that she had no choice but to meet his eyes, eyes that had gone as dark as the sea at night. 'By Allah,' he whispered, 'it is a scent more sweet than any I have ever known.'

He bent and kissed her throat again. Joanna's eyes closed and she swayed in his arms, hating herself for whatever weakness it was that possessed her when he touched her, hating him even more for finding that weakness and exploiting it.

'The only name I'd ever call you is bastard,' she said unsteadily. 'And—and that would be only the beginning.'

Khalil laughed softly. 'Has no one ever taught you manners?'

'No one's ever tried to tell me how to live my life, if that's what you mean!'

She had meant to insult him, but her words only made him grin. 'Ah. We're back to that, are we? Khalil the dictator.'

'We never left it! You think—you think you can——'

'The first thing you must learn,' he said, 'is not to talk so much.'

His mouth dropped to hers. She had been expecting the kiss, steeling herself against it, and she went rigid at the first touch of his lips. But his kiss was like a whisper—gentle, almost soft—and it sent a swift *frisson* of pleasure shimmering through her blood.

Don't, she began to say. But the thought never became a word. Instead, it emerged a sigh against his mouth. Khalil's arms went around her and he gathered her so closely to him that Joanna couldn't tell whose heart it was she felt racing, whose skin it was she felt blazing with heat.

His teeth caught her bottom lip and he drew the soft flesh into the warmth of his mouth.

'Joanna,' he whispered.

He swept the robe from her shoulders and the lightly knotted towel fell to her waist. He drew back, just far enough so he could see her. Her skin was flushed, her breasts full and hardened with desire.

'How beautiful you are,' he said, his voice thick.

Joanna felt as if the room was spinning around her. 'Please,' she whispered, 'please...'

'What? What do you want me to do, Joanna?' He reached out blindly, his fingers trailing across her collarbone, and she caught her breath. 'This?' he said softly, his eyes on her face. He touched the rise of her breast, circling the aureole lightly. Joanna whimpered and now it was he who caught his breath. 'Or this?' he said, bending his head and putting his mouth to her flesh.

She moaned, would have fallen, but he caught her and gathered her fiercely to him, his hands cupping her bottom, lifting her into the hardness of his arousal.

'Joanna,' he whispered, his voice unsteady, and she moved blindly against him, exulting in the hard feel of him, her flesh on fire...

'No!' The strangled cry burst as much from her heart as from her throat. What was he doing to her? She wasn't the sort of woman who fell into bed with a stranger or with a man she loathed! Joanna slammed her hands against Khalil's chest and pushed him away.

'All right,' she said, her breathing swift, 'you've convinced me. You're bigger than I am, and stronger, and— and——' She closed her eyes, then opened them, determined to face her humiliation without flinching. 'And there's something you do that—that makes me—makes me receptive. But——'

'Receptive?' He laughed, and whatever unsteadiness she'd thought she'd heard in his voice was gone, replaced by smug satisfaction at her embarrassment. 'What you are, my charming Miss Bennett, is ready and willing.' Her hand flashed up but he caught it before she could slap him. 'But, of course, you'd have to be, wouldn't you, to have had any hope of carrying out your little scheme?'

'I hate you,' Joanna said through her teeth. 'Do you understand? I hate you, and I'd sooner die than——'

'Yes. So you said, several times.' His smile was chill. 'It must be difficult, trying to play the part of the seductress and the wounded innocent at the same time.'

'You'll pay for what you've done, when my father comes for me, I promise you that.'

'The sooner, the better,' Khalil said grimly, thrusting her from him. 'Rachelle will bring you clothing. Then she will show you the areas in which you will be free to walk.'

'Free? You don't know the meaning of the word!'

'Behave yourself and things will not be as difficult as you imagine,' he said, striding to the door.

'And if I don't?' She flung her defiance after him, some inner need more desperate than fear spurring her on. 'What then? Will you put me in chains?'

He turned and looked at her. 'Only a stupid man would resort to such measures, Joanna.' A quick smile flashed across his lips. 'Especially when there are ones that would please me far better.'

The door opened, then shut, and Joanna was alone.

CHAPTER SEVEN

'I HAVE brought you some lunch, Joanna.'

Joanna looked up as Rachelle entered the bedroom and set a tray on the table beside the window.

'You will like it, I think. There is *kofta* and *ommu-'ali*—little meatballs—and then some rice pudding, and——'

'Thank you, but I'm not hungry.'

The bright smile dimmed. 'But you haven't even looked at it!'

'I'm sure it's delicious. But I don't want it.'

'Joanna, please. You must eat.'

'Why?' Joanna's attempted good humour vanished in a haze of frustration and disappointment. 'Is that what the Prince said?'

Rachelle flushed. 'The Prince will be concerned about the welfare of his guest.'

'Ah. That's touching. Unfortunately for me, I am not exactly his guest.'

'He will be displeased with me.'

'Send him to me, then. I'll tell him you have nothing to do with my not eating. Perhaps he needs to be reminded that prisoners often lose their appetites—but then, what would a kidnapper and bandit know about such things?'

'Hush!' Rachelle's eyes were wide with shock. 'You must not say that of my lord!'

'Why? Will he have me beaten if I speak the truth? Will he have you beaten for listening to it?' Joanna got to her feet and stalked across the room. 'Why don't you stop defending him? There's no one here but me—you can be honest for once. Your mighty Prince is nothing but a——'

Rachelle gasped, turned, and all but flew to the door.

'Rachelle!' Joanna's voice rose in dismay. 'Rachelle, wait, please! Don't go. I just wanted to——'

It was too late. The door swung shut, and she was alone again. She stared at it for a few seconds, and then she flung out her arms in frustration.

'How could you be so stupid, Joanna?' she demanded of the silent room.

She flung herself into a chair and stared blankly at the wall. She'd lost her temper with a slip of a girl who was too terrified of Khalil and the life-or-death power he held over her and the rest of his people ever to question what he did.

More importantly, she'd lost the chance to ask the only question that mattered. When would she be set free? Surely Khalil had heard from her father by now? Sam must be working as quickly as he could to meet the demands for her release, but——

A knock sounded at the door, as if in answer to Joanna's thoughts. She sprang to her feet, her heart pounding—but it was only Rachelle again, this time bearing an armful of what looked like bright lengths of fabric.

'I have brought you some things to wear,' she said, hurrying to the bed, her eyes downcast. Garments fell across the blankets, along with a pair of embroidered leather slippers. 'I hope they are to your liking, Joanna. If they are not——'

'Rachelle—I'm sorry if I insulted you before.'

The girl looked up. 'It was my lord you insulted, not me.'

'Yes.' Joanna sighed. 'And I suppose it's a capital offence to do that here, isn't it?'

Rachelle's brow furrowed. 'Capital offence? I do not understand.'

Joanna smiled tightly. 'No, I'm sure you don't.'

'The clothing,' the girl said, gesturing to the bed. 'I had to guess at the size, but——'

'I won't need it.'

Rachelle shrugged her shoulders. 'I thought you would be more comfortable in these things than in the jellaba, but if you prefer to wear it——'

'I won't be here long enough to bother changing what I'm wearing.'

The girl's eyes met Joanna's, then skittered away. 'It will not hurt to have these things,' she said.

'There's no point,' Joanna said firmly. 'Surely, by now, Khalil has heard from my father, and...' She stared at the other girl. 'He has, hasn't he?'

Rachelle seemed to hesitate. 'I do not know.'

'Khalil said he'd contacted him. Did he tell me the truth?' Rachelle's face grew shuttered and Joanna's voice sharpened with impatience. 'Come on, Rachelle, surely you can answer a simple question. Does my father know what's happened to me?'

The girl nodded. 'Yes.'

Yes. Yes. Sam knew she was being held prisoner, but he hadn't yet arranged for her release...

'I will take away the things I have brought, since you do not wish to——'

'No!' Joanna shook her head and put her hand on Rachelle's arm. 'No, leave them. On second thought, I don't want to go on wearing this—this bathrobe of Khalil's another minute.' She reached towards the bed, then stopped abruptly. 'What,' she said disdainfully, 'is this?'

'A skirt.' The girl smiled hesitantly. 'And a blouse to go with it. If they please you, I will bring you other——'

'I have no intention of wearing anything like that!'

Rachelle looked bewildered. 'Are the sizes wrong? You are so slender, Joanna, that I was not certain——'

'I'm sure the size is fine.'

'The colours, then. I thought the shade of blue was very pretty, but perhaps you would prefer——'

'A skirt that length is a mark of subservience,' Joanna said, blithely ignoring the fact that New York women were probably that minute strolling Fifth Avenue in skirts even longer than the one that lay across the bed. Her eyes flashed to Rachelle's face. 'I mean no insult,' she said quickly. 'It's only that in my country, women don't dress that way.'

'Then you will go on wearing the jellaba?'

Suddenly, the weight of the jellaba seemed unbearable against her naked skin.

'No,' Joanna said quickly.

Rachelle looked bewildered. 'Then what will you wear?'

What, indeed? Joanna gave the first answer that came into her head.

'Trousers,' she said, taking an almost perverse delight in the shock she saw in Rachelle's eyes.

'Trousers? But——'

'I know. Women don't wear them in Jandara.' Her chin lifted. 'But I am not Jandaran, Rachelle. Be sure and give that message to your high and mighty Prince.'

It was a pointless gesture, Joanna knew. Even if, by some miracle, women's trousers could be found in Jandara, surely Khalil would never agree to permitting his hostage to wear something so Western.

An hour later, Rachelle appeared at the door carrying another armload of clothing.

'I hope these things suit you better,' she said, dumping everything on the bed.

Joanna waited until the girl left, and then she walked to the bed and poked at the garments lying across it. A smile curved across her lips. There were two pairs of trousers—soft, cotton ones—and a stack of shirts, as well.

She picked one up. This was men's clothing, not women's. Everything would be too large, but what did that matter? She wasn't trying to be a fashion plate and besides, getting such things past Khalil seemed like a victory. Perhaps Rachelle had taken pity on her; perhaps she'd got the items on her own, without seeking his permission.

Quickly, Joanna stripped off the jellaba. She pulled on a pair of trousers, then slipped a navy cotton T-shirt over her head.

It was Khalil's, she thought instantly, as the soft fabric brushed past her nose. The T-shirt, the trousers—they were all his. The garments were all clean and fresh, but they bore a scent compounded of the mountains and the wind and the stallion he rode... His scent.

A tremor went through her and she closed her eyes, remembering the endless ride to this mountain stronghold, remembering the feel of Khalil's arms as he'd held her before him on the saddle.

Joanna gave herself a little shake. Impatiently, she yanked the shirt down hard over her breasts. His scent, indeed! The T-shirt smelled of the soap it had been washed with and the sunshine that had dried it, nothing more. Honestly, if she didn't get out of this prison soon...

There was a light rap at the door. She spun towards it.

'Rachelle? Thanks for bringing me this stuff. It's just too bad it belongs to your almighty Prince, but——'

'I assure you, Joanna,' Khalil said with a cool smile, 'none of it is contaminated.'

Joanna's cheeks flamed. 'I thought you were Rachelle.'

He nodded as he shut the door after him. 'Obviously,' he said drily. His gaze flickered over her slowly, and then a smile curved across his lips. 'I am sorry I had nothing more to your liking.'

'This is fine,' she said stiffly.

His eyes darkened. 'I agree,' he said softly. 'That shirt has never looked quite as good on my body as it looks on yours.'

The colour in her face deepened. She was wearing no bra—she had none to wear—and she knew that he must be able to see the rounded outline of her breasts clearly beneath the soft cotton of the T-shirt, see the prominence of her nipples, which were hardening as he looked at her.

'Clothing is clothing,' she said, her voice chill. 'Nothing more.'

His smile tilted. 'Even when it belongs to the enemy?'

Joanna's chin lifted. 'If you've come here to taunt me——'

Khalil sighed. 'I came because Rachelle says you are distressed.'

She stared at him. 'Distressed? *Distressed*?' Joanna laughed. 'Don't be absurd! Why should I be distressed? After all, here I am, the guest of the great Hawk of the North, having an absolutely wonderful time——'

'I take it you are not pleased with out efforts at hospitality.'

'I just told you, I love it here! Especially the security. Armed guards at the door—how much safer could a guest feel?'

Khalil put his hands on his hips. 'Will you promise not to try and escape if I call off the guards?' He laughed at the look on her face. 'No. I didn't think so.'

'Would you really expect me to make such a promise?'

'I have not come here to debate, Joanna. Rachelle says——'

'Rachelle says! For God's sake, if you want to know what I think, why don't you ask me? I don't need Rachelle as my interpreter!'

A smile twisted at his lips. 'I agree. You have no difficulty speaking your mind.'

'So, what do you want to know?' She gave him a beaming smile. 'Is Room Service treating me OK? Do I like the accommodation? The view?' Her mouth narrowed. 'The shackles on the walls?'

He laughed. 'The only thing I see on the walls are paintings.'

'You know what I mean, Khalil! When are you going to let me out of this prison?'

Khalil's face darkened. 'Your freedom is in your father's hands, not mine.'

Joanna looked at him and tried to keep the sudden desperation she felt from showing in her eyes.

'Well?'

'Well, what?'

'Well, when is he coming for me?'

He hesitated. 'I do not know.'

'You do not know?' Joanna said, her voice mimicking his. 'How could that be? You said you'd contacted him.'

'Yes, of course.'

'And?'

'And he has not replied to my message.'

She shot him a cold look. 'That's very hard to believe!'

Khalil's mouth narrowed. 'I am not a liar, Joanna.'

Wasn't he? He had lied well enough to lure her into the desert and carry her here...

No. She'd lied the night they'd met, not he. He'd simply made the most of things. Besides, what would he gain by lying to her now? He had sent Sam a message and Sam—and Sam had not responded...

Sudden despair overwhelmed her. She felt the unwanted sting of tears in her eyes and she started to turn away, but before she could, Khalil stepped quickly forward and clasped her shoulders.

'Joanna?'

She looked up. There was an unreadable expression on his face, something that might almost approach concern. It startled her—until she realised he would have to have some interest in her emotional condition. The last thing he'd want on his hands was an hysterical captive.

'Don't worry, Khalil,' she said with a brittle smile. 'I've no intention of making a scene. I was only thinking that if you really did ask my father to withdraw from the mining deal, you have asked for a great deal.'

A muscle knotted in his cheek. 'Perhaps. But I promise you, I have not asked him for more than you are worth, Joanna.'

She felt a flush rise over her body. How did he manage to do this to her? When he looked at her like this, everything seemed to fade into the background—everything but him, and the awareness of him that he made her feel. It was perverse. It was impossible. And yet——

He bent his head and touched his mouth to hers. The kiss was soft, almost tender, and yet she felt the heat of it race through her blood and confuse her senses.

'Joanna,' he whispered, and his lips took hers again.

She swayed unsteadily and his hands clasped her more tightly, lifting her on tiptoe, moulding her body to his while their mouths clung together. It was Khalil who finally ended the kiss. When he did, Joanna stared at him, her lips parted, her breathing swift. She wanted to say something clever and sharp, something that would put what had just happened into chill perspective—but it was Khalil who did it instead.

'Your father is not a fool,' he said, with a little smile. 'He will do what any man in his right mind would do for you.'

Of course. Any man would meet the ransom demands of his daughter's kidnappers, and Sam was no exception.

Joanna forced a thin smile to her lips. 'You don't have to tell me that, Khalil. I know it. My father will pay what you ask—but you'll never have time to enjoy it. Not when you're going to be rotting in one of Abu's prisons.'

His hands fell away from her. 'Ah, Joanna, Joanna. Whenever I begin to wonder if your spirits are sagging, you say something sweet and loving and reassure me that you're the same soft-hearted creature you've always been!'

'That's the difference between us,' she said. 'You need reminding—but I never for a moment forget what an impossible bastard you are!'

His eyes went dark. 'You play with fire, Joanna.'

'What's the matter? Can't you handle the truth? Or do you expect me to bow and scrape and worship you adoringly, the way Rachelle does?'

To her surprise, he burst out laughing. 'You? Bowing and scraping? It is an interesting thought, Joanna, but I think the only things you will ever scrape will be the chicken coops.'

'What?' She moved after him as he turned and started for the door. 'Never,' she said, 'not in this lifetime...' the door opened '...or any other,' she finished, but it was too late. Khalil was gone.

After a moment, she sighed and walked to the window. Why had she wasted time letting him bait her? There were things she'd meant to ask him, things that would make whatever time she had to spend here more bearable.

There was an enclosed garden just outside, a handsome one, from what she could see of it. Would he permit her to walk in it? Surely, he didn't intend to keep her locked up in——?

A flash of colour caught her eye. Joanna leaned forward. A little girl dressed in jeans, sneakers, and a pale blue polo shirt was playing with a puppy. Despite her own worries, Joanna began to smile. There was something about children and small animals that never failed to move her.

The child laughed as she held out a bright yellow ball, then tossed it across the grass. The puppy wagged its tail furiously, charged after the ball, and brought it back. Joanna's smile broadened. The two were having a wonderful time, judging by the way the girl was laughing. The puppy looked as if it were laughing, too, with its pink tongue hanging out of its mouth.

Joanna tucked her hip on to the window sill and watched, chuckling softly as the game continued, until the ball bounced crazily on the cobblestoned pathway, tumbled into the dark green hedge that bordered it, and vanished.

The puppy searched, as did the little girl, but neither had seen where the ball had gone.

Joanna tapped the window pane. 'There,' she said, 'in the hedge.'

Neither the child nor the dog could hear her.

She tapped the window again. If the girl would just look up...

The child's face puckered. She plopped down in the grass, snatched the puppy to her breast, and began to sob. The puppy licked her face but the child only cried harder as she rocked the animal in her arms.

Joanna turned from the window, hurried to the door, and flung it open. The guard standing outside looked up, startled.

'Excuse me,' she said, brushing past him.

He called out after her, his equivalent, she was certain, of 'Hey, where do you think you're going?' but she was already halfway down the hall, heading towards an arched doorway that she knew must open on to the garden. She went straight through it, pausing only long enough to be sure the child was still sitting in the same place, holding her dog and weeping.

'Don't cry,' Joanna said when she reached her. The little girl looked up, her eyes widening with surprise. Joanna smiled and squatted down beside her. 'Do you understand me? You mustn't cry so hard. You'll make yourself sick.'

The child raised a tear-stained face. 'Who are you?' she said, in perfect English.

'My name is Joanna. And who are you?'

'I am Lilia.' The tears began rolling down her plump cheeks again. 'And I've lost my ball!'

Joanna took the girl's hands in hers. 'It's not the end of the world,' she said softly.

'It was a special ball. My father gave it to me, and——' The tears came faster and faster. 'And he's never coming back!'

Joanna rose to her feet. 'In that case,' she said, 'we'll just have to get that ball, won't we?'

She spotted not one guard but several hurrying towards her. Too bad, she thought defiantly, as she hurried towards the hedge that had swallowed the child's toy. When she reached it, she saw that the foliage was denser than it had seemed from her window. She hesitated, then shook her head over her foolishness. It was only a hedge, and the guards were almost upon her. Quickly, she plunged her hand deep into the bush's green heart.

'Joanna!'

The ball was here somewhere, dammit. If she could just——

'Joanna! Stop it! Do you hear me?'

There! She had it now. She winced as she felt something needle-sharp hit her hand, but what did it matter? Face flushed with triumph, she pulled the yellow ball from the tangle of branches and looked up into the dark, angry face of Khalil.

'Relax, Your Highness,' she said coolly. 'I'd love to escape, but I doubt if burrowing through some shrubbery will get me very far.'

'You fool.' He barked something at Lilia, who had followed after Joanna. The little girl wiped her eyes, dropped a curtsy, and ran off with the puppy at her heels.

Joanna's eyes flashed. 'You see? Everyone bows and scrapes to you, even a slip of a child who——'

Khalil grabbed the ball from her and tossed it aside. 'Would you risk everything for something as stupid as a child's toy?'

'I know a little girl's tears mean nothing to you, oh great one, but then, you're not exactly known for having a heart, are you?' Her chin tilted. 'What now? Do I get flogged? Put on bread and water?'

Khalil snatched her wrist. 'Look,' he growled, lifting her hand.

She looked. There was a single puncture mark in the flesh between her thumb and forefinger.

'So?' Joanna's mouth narrowed. 'Don't tell me all this rage is over my getting scratched by a thorn.'

'No thorn did that, you little idiot! Do you see any thorns on that bush?'

'So what? It's nothing but a little cut. What's the matter, Khalil? Are you afraid I'll sue you?'

'Damn you, Joanna.' He caught hold of her shoulders and shook her. 'Someone should teach you that a smart answer isn't always a wise answer!'

'It won't kill me,' she said coldly. 'I assure you, I've survived worse.'

'You fool,' he said sharply. 'When will you learn to shut up long enough to listen?'

'If you're finished, I'd like to return to my room.' Her teeth flashed in a tight smile. 'Even being locked inside those miserable four walls is preferable to standing here and dealing with you!'

A muscle knotted in Khalil's jaw. 'I couldn't agree more.'

'Well, then,' she said, and turned away from him. But she hadn't taken a step before he caught hold of her and swept her up in his arms.

'Put me down!' Joanna pounded her fist against his shoulder as he strode through the garden and into the coolness of the house. 'Are you deaf, Khalil? I said, put me down!'

'With pleasure,' he growled through his teeth. 'The instant I am done with you, I will do just that.'

'What do you mean?' She pounded on his shoulder again as he swept down the corridor past her room. 'Dammit, where are you taking me?'

He glanced down at her, his eyes shimmering like the heat waves on the desert.

'To my rooms,' he said, with a smile as cold as any she had ever imagined.

Before she could answer, he shouldered open a huge wooden door, then kicked it closed behind him.

Joanna glimpsed a high ceiling, a tapestried wall, and a massive, canopied bed—and then Khalil dumped her on to the mattress, put his hands on his hips, and glared down at her.

'Now, Joanna,' he said, 'let's get down to business.'

CHAPTER EIGHT

KHALIL was angry, angrier than he should have been, considering the circumstances, but what man wouldn't be angry when an educated, intelligent woman insisted on making a damned fool of herself?

'The woman is trying to escape, Highness,' one of his people had cried out, bursting into the library just as he'd begun a strategy session with his ministers.

His men had let her run when they'd realised she had made for the enclosed garden from which there was no escape.

'I'll get her,' Khalil had said, tight-lipped, but instead of chasing down a fleeing Joanna Bennett, he'd stumbled upon a foolish one, up to her silken elbows in a shrub she should have known better than to touch in the first place.

No. That was ridiculous. Even he had to admit that. How could she have known that the seemingly innocent shrub could conceal a venomous insect? It was obvious she hadn't been trying to run away, even though he knew she could hardly wait to see the last of him.

His teeth ground together. Then why was his temper so close to boiling point? He glared down at her. He knew she prided herself on maintaining self-control but in this moment she was as transparent as glass. Looking into her green eyes, he could see her indignation and anger giving way to something else. To fear—and to the bone-deep determination not to let him see that fear.

Instantly, he realised how his sharply spoken words must have sounded. His glare deepened. Did the woman really think him such a savage that he would take her in violence, in some barbaric, retaliatory rage? His nostrils flared with distaste. He would tell her that she was a fool, that he had never in his life forced a woman into his bed and that she was not a woman he would choose to have in his bed, even if she came willingly...

... But then he looked at the glossy auburn hair that lay tumbled over her shoulders, at the rapid rise and fall of her breasts beneath the ridiculously oversized T-shirt she'd insisted on wearing, and it was as if a fist knotted suddenly in his gut. His gaze fell to her mouth, soft as a flower and slightly parted, as if a breeze had disturbed its petals. Desire raged through him, as hot as the fire that sometimes followed a strike of summer lightning in the mountain forests, hardening his groin with a swiftness that stunned him.

What nonsense was this? He was not a boy, given to uncontrollable bursts of adolescent desire. And she was not a woman he would ever want. She was clever and beautiful, yes, but she was soft and spoiled, selfish and stubborn and altogether unyielding.

And yet, she had yielded to him, when he'd kissed her. Each time he had taken her in his arms to humble her, she had instead kindled a fire in his blood, then matched it with a scorching heat of her own.

His breathing quickened. What would happen if he came down on the bed beside her? It was what she expected, he knew, that he would take her now. What would she do if he did? Would she fight him? Or would she ignite with a quicksilver flame under his touch?

'Joanna,' he said, his voice a little thick, and instantly she rose up on her knees and bared her small, white teeth.

'Go on,' she taunted, 'do whatever you're going to do. It's all the excuse I need to claw out your eyes!'

So much for her igniting under his touch! Khalil burst out laughing.

'If you claw out my eyes,' he said reasonably, 'how will I attend to you properly?'

'You couldn't,' she said. 'I mean, you can't. There's nothing you could do that would make me . . .'

'Relax, Joanna.' The look he gave her was cool, almost disinterested. 'I assure you, I've no designs on your body.'

Her face coloured. 'Then why——?' Her voice rose as he strode into the adjoining bathroom. She could hear water running, cabinet doors opening and closing, and then he reappeared, bearing a small tray arrayed with a small basin, a bottle, cotton pads, and adhesive tape. Joanna's eyes lit with suspicion. 'What's all that for?' she demanded.

He sighed dramatically as he put the tray on the bedside table and rolled back his sleeves.

'I hate to disappoint you,' he said. 'I know you're convinced I'm about to subject you to some ancient and terrible ritual.' He dipped a cotton pad into the basin. 'But I'm not planning anything more exotic than cleaning your hand.'

She jerked her hand back as he reached for it but his fingers curled around her wrist like a vice.

'Come on, Khalil, give me a break! Surely, we're too old to play Doctor.' Her breath hissed through her teeth as he dabbed the pad against her skin. 'Hey! That hurts.'

'Not as much as it will if the bite isn't tended. Hold your arm to the light, please.'

'It's nothing,' she said impatiently. 'No one dies from——'

'You may be an expert on many things, Joanna, but you are hardly one on the flora and fauna of my country. The spider that bit you might well be poisonous.'

'Poisonous?' she said stupidly. 'Hey! Hey, what are you doing?'

'Drawing out the venom.' The breath caught in her throat as he lifted her hand to his mouth. A shudder went through her as she felt the tug of his lips, the light press of his teeth, and then he dropped her hand into her lap and strode into the bathroom. She heard water running in the sink and she closed her eyes, fighting for control, but she could still feel the imprint of his mouth, the heat of it . . .

'Joanna? Are you feeling faint?'

Her eyes flew open. 'I told you, it's just a bite. I'm not . . .' She frowned as he uncapped a bottle and dampened a cotton pad with its contents. Her breath hissed as he applied it to her skin. 'Ouch. That stings! What is it?'

'An ancient medication known only to shamans and holy men.' He looked up, and she could see laughter in his eyes. 'It is peroxide, Joanna. What did you think it was?'

'How should I know?' she said stiffly.

Khalil worked in silence for a moment, and then he looked at her again.

'My men think you were trying to escape.'

'I told you, I'd be delighted to escape,' she said with a quick, cool smile. 'But I'm not stupid enough to escape into your garden.'

He laughed softly. 'No. I did not think so.'

She watched as he bent his head and began dabbing at the tiny bite mark again.

'What were you doing, then?'

Joanna shrugged her shoulders. 'The little girl lost her ball. I saw where the ball landed but she didn't, and when she started to cry——'

'Her crying annoyed you?'

'Annoyed me? Of course not. I felt sorry for her. One minute she'd been laughing and the next——' She caught her breath as he ran a finger lightly over her skin.

'The bite will itch, for a day or two,' he said, 'but it will be fine after that.'

'Fine.' Her voice shook a little and he looked up, frowning.

'What is it, Joanna? Does it hurt when I touch you there?'

'No,' she said quickly. 'It doesn't hurt at all.'

What it did, she thought wildly, was send a wave of sensation along her nerve-endings. The feeling was—it was . . .

'That's great,' she said, snatching her hand away. 'Thank you. I'm sure I won't——'

Khalil clasped her hand in his again. 'I am not done,' he said. 'I want to put some ointment on your hand and then bandage it.'

'It's—it's not necessary. Really.'

'Just hold still, please. I'll try and be more gentle.' His hands moved on her lightly, without pressure. 'It will only take another minute.'

Joanna sat beside him, her spine rigid, as he smoothed a healing cream over her slightly reddened flesh. He would try and be more gentle, he'd said—but he was already being more gentle than she could ever have imagined. She had no doubt that those large, competent hands could tame the wildest desert horse; that they could also stroke her as if his fingers were satin and her skin silk came as a surprise. He was touching her with such care, as if she were too delicate for anything but the most careful caress.

Her breathing quickened. Khalil's head was bowed over her hand. She could see the way his dark hair curled lightly over the nape of his neck, as if it were kissing his tanned skin. The fingers of her free hand tightened against her palm. What would his hair feel like, if she were to touch it? And what would he do, if she reached out and lightly stroked that ebony silk?

Some time between the last time she'd seen him and now, he'd changed his clothes. Gone was the white jellaba; in its place was a very American blue denim shirt and jeans. It was amazing, she thought, how little he looked like a fierce mountain bandit and how much he looked like a man who could walk down a New York street without drawing attention to himself—except that he would always draw attention, wherever he went. He was too self-assured, too ruggedly handsome not to be noticed.

Joanna bit down lightly on her lip. Moments ago, he'd dumped her on this bed and stood over her, fury gleaming in his eyes, and she'd thought he was going to force her to submit to him. The thought had terrified her—and yet, if she were brutally honest, she'd had some other far, darker reaction deep within herself as she'd looked up at him.

What if she'd opened her arms to him? Would the fire of anger have left his eyes and been replaced, instead, by the shine of desire? Her lashes fell to her cheeks and she imagined the feel of his body against hers, the excitement of his possession...

Dear God! Joanna's eyes flew open. She really was going over the edge! She wasn't a woman who wanted to be taken against her will any more than he was a man who would take a woman in that fashion. Why would he, when surely any woman he wanted would come to him willingly, when any woman in her right mind would turn to flame in his arms...?

'There,' he said briskly. He capped the bottle, put it on the tray, and rose to his feet. 'That should do it. The next time you want to do something heroic——'

Joanna blew out her breath. 'I wasn't being heroic. I told you, Lilia was crying, and I——'

There was a light knock on the door. 'My lord?' a little voice whispered, and Lilia stepped carefully into the room. She looked from Joanna to Khalil, who folded his arms over his chest in that arrogant posture Joanna had come to recognise. 'I am sorry, my lord,' the child said.

He nodded, his face stern. 'As well you should be.'

Joanna stood up. 'Khalil!'

'Will the lady be all right, my lord?'

'I'm fine,' Joanna said quickly.

Lilia nodded, but her attention was centred on Khalil. 'I really am sorry.' She sniffed, then wiped her hand under her nose. 'I didn't mean——'

'What you mean is, you didn't think.'

'Khalil,' Joanna said, 'for goodness' sake, tell the child that——'

'You have a place to play, Lilia. A safe place, with swings and toys—and with a nursemaid to watch over you.' Khalil's brows drew together. 'You ran away from Amara again, didn't you?'

The child hesitated. 'Well——'

'Tell me the truth, Lilia!'

'Amara fell asleep,' she said, hanging her head. 'She ate her lunch and then she ate most of a box of sweets and then she said she would just sit in the sun and rest...'

The child's mouth twitched. Joanna's eyes flashed to Khalil's face. Astonished, she watched his mouth begin to twitch, too, and then he squatted, held out his arms, and grinned.

'Come and give me a hug, you little devil,' he said. 'I haven't had one in days.'

Lilia laughed as he swung her into his arms. 'I love you, Uncle,' she said.

Uncle? *Uncle*?

He kissed the child on both cheeks, then set her on the floor and gave her a light pat on her bottom.

'Go on,' he said gently. 'Find your puppy and play some other game. I shall speak to Amara.'

'You won't be angry at her?'

He sighed. 'No.'

Lilia smiled. 'Thank you,' she said, and then she turned to Joanna. 'And thank you, for finding my ball.'

Joanna smiled, too. 'You're very welcome.' The child skipped out the door and Joanna cleared her throat. 'I didn't expect——' Khalil looked at her. 'I, um, I never imagined... I didn't know Lilia was your niece.'

'It's an honorary title,' he said.

'She's very fond of you.'

'Yes.' His expression was impassive. 'It is many years since any of us ate children for breakfast, Joanna.'

She flushed. 'I never meant to imply that you—that your people...'

'No.' His expression grew cold and forbidding. 'That's true enough. You never "imply". Why should you, when you are a veritable expert on our behaviour and customs?'

'Look, I suppose I deserved that. But you can't blame me for—for...' She sighed. 'She's a sweet little girl,' she said, after a minute.

Khalil nodded. 'I agree. She's the daughter of Amahl. He was one of my closest advisors.'

'I've never seen——'

'And you won't.' He snatched up the tray of first-aid equipment and stalked to the bathroom, Joanna trailing after him. 'Amahl was killed during a skirmish.' He yanked open the cabinet door and began slamming the first-aid equipment into it. 'Lilia was alone to start with—her mother died in childbirth—but after Amahl's death she had no one.'

Joanna could see the muscles knotting in his shoulders. Her throat tightened. She wanted to reach out, to touch him, to stroke away the tension that held him prisoner and tell him it was all right...

Prisoner? She was the prisoner, not he! She was——

Khalil swung around and faced her. 'Abu is evil, Joanna.' His voice was harsh. 'If your father signs this contract with him, it will ensure that he has enough money to buy the arms he needs to defeat us!'

She stared at him, her eyes wide. The bathroom was mirrored, and she could see their faces in its silvery walls. Khalil's and hers, their reflections seeming to slip into infinity.

What was reality and what was not?

'Abu is the Sultan of Jandara,' she whispered.

'He is a tyrant, and your father knows it.' Khalil reached out and clasped her shoulders. 'He knows it, and yet he would fatten Abu's coffers.'

'You're lying!'

'I told you, Joanna, I do not lie.'

Joanna drew a deep breath. 'I don't understand. How can he be the rightful leader of Jandara if——?'

'*I* am the rightful leader of Jandara! Abu snatched the throne from me when I was a boy.' His face darkened, and she gasped as his fingers bit into her flesh. 'My parents died in a plane crash when I was only a child. Abu and a council of elders were to rule until I came of age. Instead, he killed the elders he couldn't corrupt and seized absolute power.'

Joanna shook her head. 'If he did that, why did he let you live?'

Khalil smiled grimly. 'Perhaps because I would be more dangerous dead, as a martyr, than I am alive.'

'Then—then why haven't you done something? Why haven't you taken back the throne?'

'There is a war raging here, Joanna! You haven't seen it because it isn't the kind that's fought on great battlefields, or with planes and tanks. We meet the enemy when we can find him, we inflict damage—and wait for the day we can destroy him without destroying ourselves.' His mouth twisted. 'I cannot let my men offer their lives for me unless I am certain we can win.'

Joanna stared into Khalil's burning eyes. She wanted to believe him—but if she did, then her father would be the liar. He would be a man who had knowingly struck a deal with a tyrant...

Joanna drew a shaky breath. 'You talk about morality—and yet you deny me my freedom.' She ran the tip of her tongue over her lips. 'If you want me to believe you—if you're telling me the truth, let me go.'

Khalil's face darkened. 'It is out of the question.'

'You see? You make speeches about what is right, but...' She wrenched free of him. 'It's impossible. You stole me, Khalil. You've locked me away, kept me prisoner...'

He said a word under his breath, clasped her shoulders, and spun her towards him.

'I took you for a reason, Joanna. I had no choice.'

'Everyone has choices! Make the right one now. Let me go.'

Their eyes met and held. 'No,' he said. 'I cannot.'

'I'll tell my father what you said about Abu, I promise.'

Khalil shook his head. 'I have spoken, Joanna. I will not free you!'

Angry colour flashed across her cheeks. 'You—you pig-headed, insolent idiot! Why should I believe anything you say?'

'Stop it, Joanna!'

'I won't stop it! You're an arrogant, imperious bastard, and I can hardly wait to see you in chains!'

She cried out as his arms swept around her. 'If you won't keep quiet, I'll silence you myself,' he said, and kissed her.

Joanna twisted wildly in his arms. 'Damn you,' she hissed against his mouth. She bit down, hard enough to draw a bead of blood, but he only laughed and gathered her closer.

'Fight me,' he said, his arms holding her like bands of steel. 'What does it matter, Joanna? Soon you will be crying out my name, moving against me and pleading with me to end this war between us in the one way we both understand.'

'No,' she said, 'that's not true!'

But it was. He wanted her, and she wanted him, and whatever remained of reason fled in Khalil's impassioned kisses, kisses that demanded her submission yet promised his in return. Joanna gave a moaning sob. She wound her arms tightly around his neck and lifted herself to him, pressing her body to his, opening her mouth to the thrust of his tongue. He growled his triumph, lifted her into his arms, and carried her to his bed.

'Joanna,' he whispered.

She looked up as he lowered her to the mattress. He smiled a little, the triumphant smile of a man who knew what he wanted and was about to have it—and, with that smile, passion drained from her bones, leaving behind cold, harsh reason.

How could she let him do this to her? How could she *help* him to do this to her? He had stolen her! She was his prisoner, denied even the right to walk free in the sunshine, and he was telling her ugly lies about her own father and now here she was, in his bed, letting him use the weakness he'd found within her, use this terrible passion she had not even known existed, to make her not just his captive but his ally. She would become not only his hostage but her own, a hostage to her own sexuality.

'Let go of me!'

She slammed her hands against his shoulders and he drew back instantly.

'You're clever,' she said bitterly, 'oh, yes, you're very clever! I have to hand you that, Khalil.' She edged upwards against the pillows, her eyes locked with his. 'If you get me to sleep with you, you can't lose! You'll have me as a playmate so long as I'm here and as an insurance policy after I'm gone.'

He rose to his full height and stared at her. 'What the devil are you talking about?'

'I suppose you're right.' Joanna swung her legs to the floor and stood up. 'It would take a stronger woman than me to watch them hang the man she'd willingly gone to bed with!'

'That's nonsense!'

'Everything my father said about you is true, especially the part about you being a—a barbarian who wants to keep his stranglehold on his pathetic little fiefdom!'

She thought, for an instant, he would strike her. The bones of face showed white through his tan, and his eyes grew dark as stones. She could see him collecting himself, marshalling control of his emotions, and finally he spun on his heels, stalked to the door, and yanked it open. A

man standing guard outside snapped to attention. Khalil
spat a command at him, and the man nodded.

He looked at Joanna. 'Come,' he said, his voice hard
as ice.

'You needn't throw me out.' She fought the desire to
run and instead strolled casually to where he stood. 'I'm
more than eager to leave.'

'I'm sure you are.' He put his hand in the small of
her back and shoved her none too gently into the hall.
'My man will keep you company while you wait.'

'Charming. But what am I to wait for?'

Khalil smiled coldly. 'Smile, Joanna,' he said. 'Your
days as a cloistered prisoner are about to come to
an end.'

CHAPTER NINE

JOANNA stood in the corridor outside Khalil's bedroom and tried to look as if she found nothing unusual in being guarded by a man wearing a head-dress, a long robe and a ferocious scowl.

Was she really going to be set free? It was dangerous to let herself believe she was—but what else could he have meant when he'd said she'd been a prisoner too long? Or something like that; she'd been so stunned by the suddenness of his declaration that she wasn't quite sure exactly what it was he'd said except to know that for the first time since he'd carried her off, she felt a stir of hope.

It would be wonderful to be free, to be away from this awful place and this terrible man. He'd stolen her and now he was feeding her lies, keeping her locked up and under guard—she'd never forgive him for that or for the other indignities he'd heaped on her. Taking her in his arms, kissing her when the last thing she'd ever want were his kisses, sparking a wild passion in her blood that she'd never before known...

'Are you ready, Joanna?'

She spun around. Khalil stood in the open doorway, seeming to fill it. He wore an open-throated white shirt and black, snug-fitting trousers tucked into riding boots. A white cloak was thrown over his shoulders.

'Oh, yes,' she said with a dazzling smile. 'All I have to do is pack my suitcases and——'

'I have no time for games,' he growled.

'No. I'm sure you don't. I'm the only one around here with time on my hands.'

He smiled tightly. 'Perhaps we should discuss the goats and chickens again.'

'Perhaps we should discuss the fact that I'm not accustomed to sitting on my hands all day.'

'Had you shown me you could behave yourself, I intended to give you greater freedom.'

'Had I shown you I could...' Joanna tossed back her head. 'I'm not Lilia, Khalil. You can't make me do your bidding by promising me a reward.'

His eyes narrowed. 'Would you prefer that I threaten you?'

'I would prefer,' she said coldly, 'that you treat me with dignity.'

'You mean, you would prefer that I treat you as if we were in your world, that I dance attendance upon you and meet your every whim with a smile?'

'Is that how you think I live my life? Like some pampered princess in a fairy-tale?'

'Don't be silly. I know better.' Khalil folded his arms over his chest. 'You go to your office at Bennettco every day and put in long, gruelling hours, working side by side with your father.' He smiled grimly. 'That's what you wanted me to believe, isn't it?'

Joanna flushed. What was the sense in pretending? 'I would have gladly put in twenty-four-hour days at the office,' she said. 'But my father is as much of a male chauvinist as you are!'

'Another crime to add to my list.' Khalil turned as one of his men came hurrying down the hall. 'Ah,' he said, taking a silver-trimmed white cloak from his hands, 'you've brought it. Thank you, Ahmed.' He held it out to Joanna. 'Put this on.'

She eyed the garment with scorn. 'I'm not one of your women. You can't wrap me up like a Christmas package!'

Khalil sighed wearily. 'I would not dream of making a Christmas package of you. You are far too prickly a gift to give anyone.'

'Good. Then you can forget about me wearing that thing.'

He stepped forward and draped the cloak about her rigid figure, drawing the hood up and over her bright auburn hair.

'You will wear it,' he said.

Joanna glared at him. 'Why?'

Khalil put his hand in the small of her back and pushed her gently ahead of him along the corridor.

'For no more devious reason than your comfort. It's cool in the mountains this time of year.' He looked at her and shook his head. 'Why must you always search for hidden meanings?'

'Dammit!' She shrugged free of his hand and swung towards him, her mouth trembling with anger. 'Anyone listening to you would think you've treated me with honesty and respect from the moment we met!'

His eyes darkened. 'I've dealt with you as you deserved.'

'Would you respect me more if I'd spent my life herding goats?'

To her surprise, a grin spread across his face. 'Are we back to that? It might be a good idea for me to have you spend the day with the goat-herders!'

'I'd rather spend it with Lilia,' she snapped. 'That poor little girl seems almost as miserable as I am.'

Khalil's smile vanished. 'I try my best to make her happy,' he said stiffly.

'She's very lonely.'

'Do you think I don't know this?' His mouth tight-ened. 'I realise that she could use companionship—but it never occurred to me that you would enjoy spending time with her.'

'No. Why would it, considering that you're so certain you know all there is to know about me? You accused *me* of trying to categorise *you*, but you've done the same thing to me from the instant we met!'

'I know what I see.'

'Really. Then I suppose you know that I like children very much, that for a while, when I was at school, I thought of studying to be a teacher.'

'You?' He smiled again. 'A teacher?'

'That's right. Me, a teacher. And I'd have been a good one, too.'

'What stopped you, then?'

Joanna hesitated. 'My father didn't approve.'

'And you changed your course of study, because of that?' Khalil's smile was open this time, and genuine. 'That's hard to believe.'

'I changed it because...' She hesitated again, un-certain of why she was telling him something she'd never told anyone. 'I thought he disapproved of teaching be-cause he wanted me to come into Bennettco.'

'But he didn't,' Khalil said softly.

Joanna shook her head. 'No. He—he just wanted me to—to——'

'He wanted you to be what I have accused you of being: a handsome accessory for a man to wear proudly on his arm.'

'Yes!'

Her head came up sharply; she was more than ready to tell him what she thought of such an attitude. But he wasn't looking at her with derision; what she saw in his eyes was nothing she understood.

'Perhaps we see only what we wish to see,' he said after a moment.

It was a strange thing for him to have said, Joanna thought. She wanted to ask him what he'd meant, but he put his arm lightly around her shoulders and they stepped out into bright sunshine. Ahead, two horses stood waiting in the cobblestoned courtyard. She recognised Najib instantly. The big stallion was pawing impatiently at the ground. But there was another horse standing beside him, a smaller, more delicate one, as white as Najib was black. Her bridle was hung with tiny silver bells, and her saddle was a masterwork of finely tooled leather.

'This is Sidana,' Khalil said, gently stroking the mare's long nose. He smiled. 'She is gentle, although even she may object if you mount from the wrong side. I promise you that she will take us safely to our destination and then back.'

Joanna looked at him. 'You're not setting me free, are you?' she said, with a sinking heart.

He shook his head. 'I am not.'

She nodded. 'I see.'

'No,' Khalil said fiercely, 'you do not see! But you will. After today, you will not believe the lies you have been told by your father.'

'What lies will I believe, then? Yours?'

The muscle in his jaw knotted with anger. 'Go on,' he said tightly, 'get on the horse.'

'This is pointless! If you really think I'm dumb enough to fall for some charade you've set up in my honour——'

'Get into the saddle, Joanna—or I'll lift you on to Najib's back and you will ride with me!'

Ride with him? Feel his arms around her, his heart beating against her back? Feel his breath warm at her temple, his thighs hard as they enclosed hers? Colour flamed in her cheeks.

'I'd sooner ride with the devil,' she muttered, and she grabbed for the pommel, stabbed her foot into the stirrup, and climbed into the saddle.

'All right?' She nodded and Khalil sprang on to Najib's back in one fluid motion. 'Hold the reins loosely but firmly, so the mare knows you're in command. You'll have no problem with her. She is sweet-tempered and obedient, and very well trained.'

'The perfect female,' Joanna said sweetly as they started from the courtyard. Behind them, two of Khalil's men and their horses fell into place at a slight distance.

Khalil laughed. 'I never thought of it that way, but now that you point it out, I suppose she is.'

'You still haven't told me where we're going.'

'You'll know the place when you see it.'

'I've no idea what that's supposed to mean.'

Khalil smiled. 'Why don't you relax, Joanna? You've complained about being cooped up—well, here's your chance to enjoy some fresh air and new sights. Look around you, and enjoy this beautiful day.'

He was right, she thought grudgingly. It was, indeed, a beautiful day. The dark green mountains pierced a sky so blue and so bright it almost hurt the eyes. It was spring, and wild flowers were beginning to carpet the gentler slopes, filling the air with their sweetness.

It was lovely here. Joanna thought of New York and Dallas, of crowded city streets thronged with people and automobiles. All of it seemed far, far away. How easy it would be to be happy in a place like this, she thought suddenly. Unbidden, her gaze flew to the man riding at her side.

What was wrong with her? Here she was, being taken out on a tether and thinking nonsensical thoughts, while somewhere her father must be agonising over her welfare.

'Listen,' she said, glaring at him, 'if you think taking me to some—some staged bit of theatre will turn my head around...'

'There is the stage, Joanna, and the players.' Khalil reached out and caught the reins of her horse. 'An hour from now, you can tell me what you think of the production.'

Before she could speak, he tapped his heels into Najib's flanks and both horses shot forward. Joanna clung to the mare's reins, too intent on what she saw to be afraid of the sudden swift motion.

They were entering a town, a real one, with houses and narrow streets. Not even Khalil could have had this place created overnight, she thought wildly as he brought their horses to a stop.

'Would you like to get down and walk around, Joanna?'

She started. Khalil had dismounted. He was standing beside the mare, looking up at her, his face as expressionless as a mask.

She nodded, too bemused to offer any objection when he held up his arms. She went into them readily, her hands light on his shoulders to steady herself, and he eased her gently to the ground.

'What is this place?' she asked.

'It is Adaba. Our central marketplace.' He took her arm and they set off along the narrow street, his two men trailing behind them. 'I thought you might like to see some of my downtrodden subjects with your own eyes.'

She wanted to make a clever retort but already her gaze was moving towards the market ahead. People were selling things and buying things, and she could hear bursts of chatter and laughter. It looked very much like the outdoor markets that flourished in lower Manhattan. People were busy. And happy. But—but...

'Observe the way my people cringe at the sight of me,' Khalil murmured.

In fact, most of the people didn't seem to notice him or, if they did, they paused in their transactions only long enough to smile and touch their foreheads.

'What did you do,' Joanna asked with a chill smile, 'tell them you'd chop off their heads if they threw themselves at your feet this one time?'

His hand tightened on her arm. 'Why be so uncreative, Joanna? Perhaps I threatened to skin them alive if they didn't behave.'

'No doubt!'

A woman came hurrying up to them. She touched her hand to her forehead but Khalil stopped her, put his arm around her shoulders, and kissed her cheek. The woman glanced shyly at Joanna and said something that made him laugh before she melted away into the crowd.

Joanna tried unsuccessfully to wrench her arm from his grasp. 'What's so funny?' she demanded. 'Or does the sight of a captive always rate a chuckle in this crowd?'

Khalil grinned. 'She wanted to assure me that even though your eyes are an interesting colour, she still prefers the blue of mine.'

'A fan,' Joanna said drily. 'How wonderful. Did she want your autograph, too?'

'Her name is Cheva. She was my nurse, when I was a boy. She loved my English mother very much, and it always pleased her that I inherited her——'

Joanna stared at him. 'Your mother was English?'

He laughed. 'Close your mouth, Joanna. It is a warm day, and there are flies about. She was, yes.' His arm slipped to her waist as he led her deeper into the crowded marketplace. 'She was an archaeologist, come to Jandara on a dig. I know you would like me to think my barbarian father abducted her, but the truth is they met at an official function, fell in love, and were married ten days later.'

'And were they happy?'

'The barbarian and the Englishwoman?'

'No,' Joanna said quickly, 'I didn't mean——'

'They were very happy. Is that so difficult to believe?'

Joanna looked at him. 'I—I'm confused,' she whispered. 'I don't—I don't really know what to believe.'

His arm tightened around her. 'Perhaps you will know, by the afternoon's end.'

When the sun began dropping in the sky, they made their way back to the horses. By then, Joanna's head was spinning. Nothing was as she'd expected—and yet, in her heart, she knew that everything was as she'd begun to suspect it might be.

She didn't speak the language of Khalil's people, but it didn't matter. Many of them spoke English, especially the younger ones.

'It is an important language, the language of nations, Prince Khalil says, so we learn it,' a horse trader told her earnestly. 'We start young, when we first enter school.'

'Ah,' said Joanna. 'Only boys learn a language, then?'

'Is that how it is in your country?' the young man said, frowning. 'That only boys may learn?'

She stared at him. 'No. Of course not. Boys and girls both learn what they wish.'

'Here, too.' He smiled. 'I am glad to hear that America believes in educating its women.'

Khalil laughed. 'I assure you,' he said, clapping the young man on the shoulder, 'it does!'

At a stall where fresh fruits lay heaped in abundance, a group of young women stood chatting.

'It must be difficult,' Joanna said to one of them, 'to raise a family here, so far from modern conveniences.'

The young woman nodded. 'It is not simple.'

Joanna's brows arched as she glanced at Khalil, who stood several feet away, lounging against a stall.

'Why don't you leave, then?' she said. Her voice fell in pitch. 'Is it because Prince Khalil will not permit it?'

The young woman repeated Joanna's words to her friends, who covered their mouths and laughed.

'We are free to leave, if we choose,' she said, turning back to Joanna. 'But only a fool would wish to live in the south, under the rule of Abu. Surely, you know this.'

Joanna stared at the woman. I don't know *what* I know, she wanted to say... But she only smiled.

'Thank you for talking with me,' she said.

She was silent when Khalil took her hand and drew her forward along the dusty street.

'Well, Joanna?' he asked softly. 'Have you seen reality?'

'It's been a long day, Khalil. I'm tired. Can we go back now, please?'

He looked at her, then nodded. 'As you wish.'

They made their way to where the horses waited. Joanna walked to the mare's side and put her hand on the animal's neck. She closed her eyes and pressed her forehead lightly against the coarse hair.

'Joanna.' Khalil's voice was gentle and so was the hand he placed on her shoulder. He said her name again but she didn't answer. After a moment, he spoke to his men. One of them reached for the mare's reins, and they led her away.

Khalil clasped Joanna's waist and lifted her on to the back of the stallion, then swung into the saddle behind her. His arms went around her as he gathered the reins into his hands, but she didn't protest. A terrible languor had crept over her.

The town fell behind them as they rode slowly towards the mountains. Finally, in a field of wild flowers, Khalil reined in the horse and slid to the ground. He looked at Joanna and held up his arms. She hesitated, then put her hands on his shoulders and dropped lightly to the ground.

'What is wrong, Joanna?'

She bowed her head, not wanting him to see the sudden dampness she knew must be glinting on her lashes, but he framed her face in his hands and lifted it to him.

'Is the truth so awful to see?' he said softly.

She shook her head again. Had she seen the truth, or had she seen illusion? It was becoming harder and harder to tell.

'Then why are you crying, Joanna?'

'I'm not,' she said, while one small tear coursed down her cheek.

He smiled a little and caught it on his fingertip. 'What is this, if not a tear?'

She sighed as she stepped away from him. Slowly, she bent and plucked a daisy from the chorus nodding at her ankles. She lowered her face to it, inhaling its sweetness, and then she stared blindly into the distance, where the mountains rose towards the sky. At last, she turned to Khalil and said what she had not even wanted to think.

'You told me the truth when you said the price of my freedom would be my father's willingness to give up his deal with Abu, didn't you?'

He nodded. 'Yes.'

Joanna swallowed hard. 'And he's refused to do it, hasn't he?'

Khalil nodded again. 'I'm sorry,' he said in a low voice. 'The only reality I wished you to see was that of my people.'

'There are many different realities, Khalil. Perhaps— perhaps it's time I finally faced my own.'

'Joanna.' She lifted her head and the hood of her cloak fell back, revealing her pale oval face and the long, fiery spill of her hair. 'I am certain he thinks I will change my mind and send you back to him.'

'And will you?' Her eyes caught his. 'Will you send me back, even though you haven't gotten what you wanted from Bennettco?'

Khalil came closer to her and cupped her face in his hands. 'How can I send you back?' he said fiercely. 'How can I do that, Joanna?'

He couldn't. She was his pawn, his bargaining chip— and, knowing that, believing she was in the hands of a man he thought a bandit and a barbarian, her father was still reluctant to do the one thing that would free her, to give up a fortune in the earth for his daughter's release.

No. No! It couldn't be! Khalil was lying. He was lying about everything.

'If there's a shred of decency in you, you'll free me,' she said.

His eyes darkened. 'I told you, I cannot.'

'You've lied to me! You haven't really contacted my father——'

'Joanna!' He took her by the shoulders. 'Listen to me.'

'My father loves me,' she said, her mouth trembling.

'In his way, I'm sure he does. But——'

'There is no "but", Khalil. Whatever you showed me today was—it was interesting, but——'

'Interesting? What do you mean, "interesting"?'

'I mean, it's interesting to—to see a little backwater town where—where people aren't living in poverty and misery, and I suppose—I suppose it must be quite a salve to your ego, hearing them talk about how wonderful you are, but that's not the whole story. There's more to it.'

'Joanna, dammit! If you won't listen to me, listen to yourself! What you're saying makes no sense.'

'No!' She flung her hands over her ears. 'I won't listen! I won't!'

'You will listen,' he said fiercely, catching her wrists and forcing her hands to her sides. 'You will, because—because...' He looked into her eyes, and then he pulled her into his arms and his mouth fell on hers.

'Don't!' Joanna pushed against his chest. 'I hate you, Khalil!'

'Liar,' he whispered, catching her mouth with his again.

'You think you can solve everything this way,' she said, twisting her face away from him. 'You think you can silence me and—and make me believe things that aren't true!'

Khalil's arms tightened around her. 'The only truth that matters is this one, this hunger that has been between us since the night we met.'

'Don't try and make it sound romantic! We met because you were determined to make it impossible for Bennettco to conduct legitimate business, and—and then you—you kidnapped me! You carried me off on your plane and——'

'And desired you, even then.' He laughed huskily. 'A hundred years ago, I would have carried you off on the back of my horse.'

'Exactly!' Joanna thrust her hands against his shoulders. 'Your ancestors were barbarians, and you——'

'My ancestors knew what they wanted and took it.' He caught her hands in his and held them against his heart. 'As I want you now—as you want me.'

'No! That's not true! I despise you, Khalil, I——'

He kissed her again, his mouth moving softly against hers.

'Despise me all you will,' he whispered, 'but do not deny me—or yourself.'

He was wrong. She was not denying anything. She didn't want this, didn't want his mouth on hers or his hand moving against her skin...

No. No, she didn't. She didn't...

Oh, God! With a desperate cry, Joanna threw her arms around Khalil's neck. He whispered her name and then his open mouth met hers in a wild kiss. His fingers speared into her hair as they sank to the ground and she fell back among the flowers, taking him with her. Khalil groaned and kissed her again and again, his mouth hot against hers.

It was as if Joanna were being swept along in a fever of desire. Her fingers flew to the neck of his jellaba, burrowed beneath his open-throated shirt. She had to touch his skin, had to feel its heat against hers or surely she would die.

Khalil lifted her to him, curving her soft body into the hardness of his. He kissed her deeply, crushing her mouth under his until she knew the taste of him would be a part of her forever.

He knelt and drew her up with him. 'Joanna,' he whispered as he slipped the white cloak and then her cotton shirt from her body. The air was cool against her skin, but his mouth and hands were hot. She caught her

breath as he cupped her breasts and when he bent and
kissed the nipples, she cried out in pleasure.

Khalil lowered her gently to the grass, then drew back.

'No,' she cried, reaching out to him—but he had only
left her so he could strip off his jellaba and then his
shirt. How beautiful he was! His skin was the colour of
honey, his muscles hard and clearly defined. He was male
perfection, and he was hers.

'Touch me,' he whispered, taking her hands in his and
bringing them to his chest.

She gasped at the feel of his skin, hot from the sun
and from desire.

'Joanna, my beautiful Joanna.' He came down beside
her and stroked his fingers along her skin, over the curve
of her breasts, down over the slight arch of her belly.
'How I want you,' he whispered, 'how I have wanted
you from the moment I saw you.'

She reached up and clasped his head, brought his
mouth to hers and kissed him, and then she smiled.

'How much do you want me?' she whispered.

A dark flush rose along his cheeks. He clasped her
hand, brought it to his mouth and bit lightly at the soft
skin below her thumb, then drew it slowly down his body,
to where his aroused flesh pressed against his trousers.
Her lashes fluttered to her cheeks as he cupped her hand
over him. His erection seemed to pulse through the cloth,
the heat of it burning her palm like flame.

'That much,' he said thickly. He bent to her and kissed
her, his tongue moving within her mouth as she knew
his body would soon move within hers.

A primitive rush of joy and desire swept through her.
This was what she wanted, what she'd wanted from the
start. Khalil, in her arms. Khalil, kissing her and
touching her and bearing her down, down into the soft,
sweet grass...

...Khalil, her captor. Her keeper. He had spoken of reality, and of truth, and yet wasn't that the one truth that mattered? She wasn't here of her own free will, she was here because one man refused to bargain for her freedom and another refused to grant it—and now she was in the arms of the man who'd caused the conflict, behaving as he'd predicted she would from the first night he'd met her.

With a cry, Joanna shoved free of Khalil's arms and scrambled to her feet, snatching up her cloak and whipping it around her, trembling with rage at him, at her father, but most of all, at herself. Khalil rose too, his eyes blurred with desire, and held out his hand.

'Joanna,' he whispered, 'what is it?'

'Who in hell do you think you are?' she said shakily. 'Treating me like—like one of your slave girls!'

His brows knotted together. 'What?'

'I've read a lot of stuff about women and—and this kind of sex,' she said, her words rushing together, 'about—about rape fantasies, but—but I never believed any of it, not for a minute, until——'

'Stop it!' Khalil's mouth twisted as he took a step towards her. 'You're talking nonsense.'

'I'm talking reality. Aren't you the one who's big on that?' Her breath was coming fast, in hard little gasps; she felt as if she'd been running for her life and it occurred to her that, in some strange way, she had been. 'I don't know how you set up today's performance in Adaba, my lord Khalil, but it doesn't matter. The point is, I've seen through it. Sam was right. You *are* a savage, and you always will be!'

He stepped forward swiftly and she flinched back, determined to show him no fear but unable to stop herself from reacting to the terrible darkness in his eyes.

'Get on the horse,' he said softly, in a voice that sent a shudder along her spine. 'Sit still and say nothing until we reach the palace.'

Joanna tossed her head. 'Certainly, my lord. Of course, my lord. Your every wish is my——'

She gasped as his hands closed on her shoulders.

'Push me, Joanna,' he growled. 'Push me, and you'll find out exactly how savage I can be.'

Her lips parted, preparatory to another quick rejoinder, but then she looked into his eyes and saw the coldness in them. The Hawk of the North, she thought, and a shudder went through her.

'That's right,' he said, very softly. 'I could do anything to you now, and no one—no one!—would ever call me to task for it. Now, turn around, get on the horse, and obey my every order. If you can do that, perhaps you'll get back to the palace safely.'

Joanna clamped her lips together defiantly, swung away from him, and did as he'd commanded. But as he swung into the saddle behind her and jabbed his heels hard into Najib's flanks, a little part of her wondered if she'd ever really be safe again.

CHAPTER TEN

JOANNA paced the confines of her room. Twenty paces to one wall, fifteen to the other, then back again. After a week, she knew the dimensions as well as she knew those of the garden, of the palace grounds, of Khalil's library. And she knew, too, that she would never again look at a caged beast without feeling a swift pang of compassion.

Not that she was being mistreated. Never that. If anything, the circumstances of her captivity had improved since that day in the meadow. Rachelle had brought her the news the following morning.

'You may walk with me where you wish, Joanna,' she'd said with a smile, 'and you may use my lord's library at will.'

Joanna's lips tightened. Perhaps Khalil had thought he could convince her he wasn't the savage she'd called him by allowing her to read his books and stroll the grounds. But he was wrong. She knew him for what he was, and nothing would ever change that now. The reality he'd wanted her to see wasn't in Adaba, it was here, in the way he kept her captive, in the way Rachelle turned pale each time Joanna dared to speak of her lord and master as the scoundrel he was.

Adaba! Joanna laughed bitterly. The dog and pony show that had been staged there only proved just how much power Khalil really wielded. Adaba had been a stage set! Oh, the thriving marketplace had probably been real enough—but the idiotically happy villagers had been straight out of Disneyworld!

137

Had Khalil bought their compliance with threats? Had he bribed them with promises? Or were the people who'd been so artfully displayed for her benefit simply among the worshipful followers that inexplicably collected around every tyrant the world had ever known, from Attila the Hun straight through to Josef Stalin?

Joanna kicked her discarded shoes out of the way and stalked the length of the room again, remembering how she'd awakened here that first morning, coming hazily out of a dream in which her father had been so busy moving a piece around a game-board that he hadn't noticed the horseman riding down on her.

'Stupid,' she muttered, flinging back her head. 'You were so stupid, Joanna!'

Her father wasn't blind to what was happening to her! He just didn't care!

No. No, that was putting things too harshly. Her father cared. It was just that he wasn't worried about her being held here. Why should he? He'd figured what she should have realised all along, that although Khalil had no hesitated to abduct her he wouldn't harm her, no matter what he threatened. He needed her to get what he wanted.

Sam had understood from day one. He had lots of time to wheel and deal and see if he couldn't come up with a way to secure her release without giving up the lucrative contract he'd worked so hard to get. So what if she'd been sitting here, docile as a clam, waiting to be rescued while Khalil spun a web of confusion around her!

Joanna spun towards the mirror on the far wall and stared at her reflection. The woman in the mirror looked well. Her cheeks had taken on a pink glow from the hours she spent in the garden. The sun had burnished her hair, and her eyes gleamed brightly.

'It is our mountain air that brings such a glow,' Rachelle had said just this morning.

Joanna smiled coldly. The girl was almost pitiably naïve. What her eyes glowed with was rage—and yet, for all her anger, she'd been able to do nothing to alter things.

But that was about to change. After days of scheming, she had finally come up with an idea that might work.

'With an idea that *will* work,' she whispered to her reflection.

God, it had to!

She took a deep breath. There was no reason to wait another minute. It was time.

Determinedly, she stabbed her feet into her shoes, then stalked to the mirror again. She peered into the glass and took half a dozen slow, deep breaths. Good. Now to relax her features. Yes. That was the way. She looked wistful, almost forlorn. Now a little tilt of the head. Not too much. Just enough to... OK. That was fine.

'It's now or never,' she said softly, and then she turned and walked to the door.

The guard in the corridor snapped to attention the instant the door swung open.

'*Ya?*'

Joanna gave him what she hoped was a tremulous smile. 'I should like to see the Prince.'

His brow furrowed and he shook his head.

'The Prince,' she said. 'Khalil.'

'*Dee Prinz?*'

'Khalil. Yes. I must speak with him.'

'Rachelle, *ya?*'

'No. I don't want to see Rachelle. I want to see your Prince.'

'*Prinz. Ya.* Rachelle.'

'Oh, for heaven's sake,' Joanna snapped, her modest smile gone in a flash, 'if everyone here speaks English what stroke of bad luck put *you* at my door?'

She elbowed past the man before he had time to react and began marching down the corridor. His voice called after her, rising in intensity, and then she heard the thud of his footfalls following her. His hand closed none too gently on her shoulder.

'Let go of me, you ape,' she snarled. 'Let go, or I'll kick you in the——'

'What is going on here?'

Joanna and the guard both swung towards the sound of that steely voice. Khalil stood in the doorway of a room just beyond them, his hands on his hips, his expression grim.

The guard began babbling an explanation, but Joanna cut it short.

'Tell your Dobermann to let go of me,' she said.

Khalil's brows rose a little, but he barked out a command and the man released her.

'Now, Joanna, suppose you tell me what you are doing here.'

'I have to talk to you,' she said stiffly. 'I told this—this creature that, but he didn't understand me.'

'Mustafa is neither an ape, a dog, nor a creature. It is hardly his fault he doesn't speak your tongue. He was told to send for Rachelle if you needed something.'

'Rachelle can't help me. Only you can do that.'

'I am busy.'

'I'm sure you are. But——'

'Speak with Rachelle,' he said as he stepped back inside the room. 'She will convey your message to——'

'Wait!' Joanna sprang forward and thrust her hand against the door. The guard sprang forward too, clasping her arm and growling a warning, and almost too late she remembered that she'd come here with every intention of playing the reserved, unhappy maiden. 'Please,' she murmured softly, and turned her face up to Khalil's with a desperation that made her stomach threaten to give up her breakfast.

But it worked. She could see the faintest softening along the hard, set line of his mouth. He stared at her for a few seconds and then he waved his hand at Mustafa, who let her go instantly.

'I will give you five minutes, Joanna.'

She nodded as he opened the door and motioned her past him. She glanced around curiously. This was his den, she thought, or——

'This is my office.'

She swung around. Khalil was standing at the closed door, looking at her.

'I didn't realise I'd spoken aloud.'

'You didn't.' Frowning, he walked quickly to a handsome old desk that stood before the window. 'But I knew you must be wondering what possible use a savage could have for a room such as this, so I decided to save you the trouble of asking.'

'I didn't come here to quarrel, Khalil.'

'Why did you come here, then?' He pushed aside a stack of papers and leaned back against the desk, his eyes cool and steady on hers. 'If it is to ask if I have had any word from your father, I have not.'

'No.' She touched the tip of her tongue to her lips. 'No, I—I didn't come for that, either.'

'What is it, then?' He frowned, pushed back the sleeve of his shirt, and looked at his watch. 'I have much to do, and little time to spare.'

You arrogant s.o.b., Joanna thought. You impossible, imperious bastard...

'Well? What was so important that you saw it necessary to push past my man and disgrace him?'

She ached to tell him that it was she who had been disgraced, from the minute she'd walked into the Oasis Restaurant almost a week ago. But she had a plan, and she was going to make it work.

'I've been thinking about something we touched on the day you took me to Adaba——'

'Nothing that happened that day is worth discussion,' he said, his face hardening. He leaned away from the desk. 'Now, if that's all——'

'I told you that I was bored, sitting around and doing nothing,' Joanna said quickly. He looked at her, and she forced herself to smile politely. 'Surely, you can understand that.'

'I have granted you the freedom of the grounds,' he said. 'And the use of my library.'

'Oh, yes. You've been very generous.'

His eyes narrowed, and Joanna groaned inwardly. Don't overdo it, she told herself. The man may be arrogant, but he's not a fool.

'Then what more do you want of me?' His look hardened. 'If you have come to ask to spend time with Lilia, I must tell you that I have changed my mind about permitting it. I do not think you would be a good influence on her.'

Joanna's chin lifted. 'No,' she said evenly, 'of course not. She's much better off in your company.'

His eyes flashed to hers and she smiled pleasantly. After a moment, he nodded stiffly towards the shelves that lined the walls.

'There are more books here, but I doubt if they would be to your liking. However, if you wish, I will tell Rachelle to bring you——'

'Thank you. But I've enough to read. I need to do something active.'

'Rachelle takes you walking each afternoon.'

Like a pet dog on a leash, she thought. 'Yes,' she said evenly, 'she does. But I need more activity than that.'

His lips drew back from his teeth. 'I wish I could help you, but, unfortunately, we haven't much to offer in the way of parties or discos.'

'Exercise,' she said, hoping he couldn't hear the sharp edge of anger in her voice. She gave him another stiff smile. 'That's what I'm talking about. I'm not used to sitting around, Khalil. When my father and I are in New York, I work out at a gym.'

'I know this will astound you,' he said, his eyes cold, 'but somehow I've not got around to having a Nautilus machine installed.'

Oh, how pompous he was, how arrogant...

'I didn't think you would have,' she said pleasantly.

'Well, then——'

'When my father and I are on our ranch outside Dallas, I ride.'

'Ride?' he said, his brows angling up in his otherwise expressionless face.

'Yes. We have horses, and——'

'You?' He laughed. 'On a horse?'

'What's so funny?' she said, the carefully drawn smile slipping from her face.

Khalil shook his head. 'Nothing much. I was just remembering how you couldn't tell the front of my horse from the rear.'

'I was upset.'

'Not as upset as Najib,' he said, chuckling. 'He must have thought he was——'

'I don't give a damn what that miserable black beast thought!' Joanna slammed her hands on her hips. 'He's not a horse, he's—he's a creature come straight out of a nightmare.'

'Like his owner,' Khalil said, very pleasantly.

'Yes! Exactly like...' She stared at him, horrified. 'No,' she said quickly. 'No, I didn't mean——'

'Stop this farce, Joanna!' His smile vanished; the stony look settled on his face again and he rose to his full height and glared at her. 'I am not for a moment going to believe that you have suddenly turned into a sweet-tempered lamb when we both know that what you are is a sharp-toothed vixen. Tell me what it is you want, and be quick about it.'

Joanna nodded. 'All right. I was quite serious when I said I was going crazy with boredom and just as serious when I said I like to ride. Don't look at me that way, Khalil! I was too upset the night you brought me here to think straight, about getting on and off your horse or anything else.'

He nodded curtly. 'Perhaps.'

'It's the truth! I didn't have any trouble the other day, did I? I didn't need you to tell me how to handle the mare.'

He scowled. 'She is docile.'

'I can ride, I tell you. And I came here to ask you to let me ride an hour a day, to——'

'It is out of the question.'

'Why?' Joanna folded her hands in front of her so he wouldn't see them tremble. If he denied her this... 'Why?' she repeated. 'I do know how! If you don't believe me, you can take me out yourself the first time, you can watch me——'

'No.' He swung away from her so she couldn't see his face and walked around the desk. 'I'm much too busy to waste time in your company, Joanna.'

The sharp words knifed into her breast, although surely what she felt was anger at his insolence, not pain at his dismissal.

'I wouldn't expect you to.'

He looked at her and smiled. 'Do you really think me so stupid, that I would let you ride by yourself?'

'What I thought was that you could let me ride with an escort.'

'It's impossible.' He sat down behind the desk, bent over some papers, and began rifling through them. 'Now, if you're done——'

'Why is it impossible?'

Khalil looked up. 'Because I said it was.'

'You could let me ride the mare—heaven knows the only thing she'd do is plod along obediently beside my guard's horse.'

'Joanna——'

Desperation made her do what she'd promised herself she would never give him the satisfaction of doing. Her eyes grew shiny with unshed tears, her mouth trembled, and when she spoke, her voice did, too.

'Please,' she whispered, 'Khalil, please! I'll—I'll die if I have to sit around like a caged bird.'

Her words drifted away and she fell silent, hating herself for having thrown herself on his mercy, hating herself even more for the real wave of despair that suddenly threatened to overwhelm her. Why was looking at him, seeing that coldness in his eyes, so agonising?

She swung away. 'I'm sorry I've wasted your time.'

His chair scraped against the floor. She heard the sound of his footsteps coming towards her, felt the weight of his hands on her shoulders.

'Joanna.' He turned her towards him. 'Look at me.' When she did, he frowned down at her. 'Is it so terrible here for you?'

'Of course it is. How do you think it feels to be a captive?'

'Yes.' His voice was low. 'That is what you are, Joanna. My captive.'

Their eyes met. A soft sound rose in Joanna's throat as she looked into the dark blue depths of his eyes. He was right. She was his captive. She belonged to him.

There was a sudden tension in the room. Her heart began to race. She remembered how he'd kissed her in the meadow, how he'd drawn her down into the soft, sweet grass, how the heat of his mouth and the heat of the sun had seemed the same...

She stepped back before he could reach for her. 'I know what I am.' Her voice was cool and steady, although her heart was still pounding. 'And if you are half the great humanitarian you claim to be, I think it's time you considered my feelings and not just your own.'

Khalil's mouth thinned. 'Is that what you think this is about?'

'I've no wish to argue the issue, Khalil. I came to ask a favour of you. Will you let me ride, or won't you?'

Long seconds passed. Then he moved past her, marched to the door, and wrenched it open. The guard stepped forward, and Khalil barked a series of orders. When he finished, he looked at Joanna.

'It is done.'

She could hardly draw breath. 'You mean—you mean, you've given permission for me to ride?'

'Once daily, and only in the company of two of my men.' His face turned stern. 'I will be away the next few days, Joanna. My men will guard you well and keep you safe.'

'They'll make sure I don't run away, you mean.'

His expression didn't change. 'I must have your word that you will never try to slip away from them.' When

she hesitated, he closed the slight distance between them
and clasped her shoulders. 'Your word, Joanna! Or I
will not permit you to ride.'

Joanna bit down lightly on her bottom lip. What did
it matter if she lied? She wasn't his guest, she was here
against her will!

'You have it,' she said.

She smiled faintly, then made her way past him and
out of the door.

'Do you speak English?' Khalil heard her say to the
guard, and when the man answered that he did, Joanna
nodded. 'We will go to the stables,' she said, as if she
had spent her entire life giving orders to men with fierce
faces and flowing robes.

Despite himself, Khalil smiled as he walked slowly to
the window. They were out in the sunshine now, Joanna
and the guard. Another of his men joined them so that
they flanked her. They were big men, better than six feet
tall, and she was a woman of average height made smaller
looking by fragile bone structure. Yet, in some strange
way, she looked every bit their equal, if not physically
then surely in determination.

And in courage. Sighing, he turned and sat down
slowly at his desk. She was not quite what he'd thought
she was, this Joanna Bennett. Khalil frowned and picked
up his pen. It would be good when her fool of a father
came to his senses and agreed to do that which had to
be done. His people would be safe, Abu would take a
step back, and Joanna—she would go back to the pretty
world in which she belonged. He would forget her in an
instant...

Certainly he would.

The pen dropped from his fingers. It seemed a long
time until he picked it up again and bent over the papers
strewn across his desk.

*   *   *

Joanna's guard seemed confused early the next morning when she opened her bedroom door and stepped out into the hall.

'I'm going horseback riding,' she said as she pushed past him and strode briskly down the corridor. She knew he couldn't understand her; knew too that she wasn't supposed to simply make her announcement and walk out, but it was all part of the painfully simple plan she'd hatched.

Pathetically simple was more like it, although now that she knew Khalil would be absent from the palace for a few days the odds of the plan working had improved. Still, everything would have to fall into place at once, if she were to make good her escape. It was why this initial attempt had to be done just this way.

Would the guard stop her?

He wouldn't, she thought with fierce exultation. He'd obviously been told she'd been granted a new privilege and now he was torn between that knowledge and whatever it was he was supposed to do next, perhaps notify the stable boy to saddle the mare, perhaps notify the men who were to accompany her that she was ready to ride.

At the door, she glanced over her shoulder. He'd finally started after her, but that was unimportant.

All that mattered was that he had let her get past him.

The next morning, she opened her door at the same hour. The guard was waiting, along with the men who'd ridden with her the prior day.

Joanna smiled. 'Good morning,' she said pleasantly. 'I was hoping Rachelle was here, with my breakfast.' She made a show of peering up and down the corridor. 'Not yet? Well, that's all right.' Still smiling, she stepped back into her room and shut the door.

At two in the afternoon, she repeated the performance of yesterday, pulling open the door, stepping past the surprised—and solitary—guard, and marching to the door. After a bewildered pause, he went trotting off in the other direction, looking, she was sure, for the men who were to ride with her.

She reached the stables first and caught the stable boy short. He was lying in an empty stall, dozing, and she had to clear her throat half a dozen times before he heard her.

Shamefaced, he sprang to his feet and said something in an apologetic tone.

Joanna smiled at him and pointed towards the mare. By the time the men who were to ride with her came scuttling into the stable, Sidana was saddled and ready.

The third day, she made her move in late morning. No one seemed too surprised this time; her erratic pattern had become the norm. That was what she'd counted on, and Khalil's absence only made things easier. Even if her guards had thought to report her, who would they have reported her to?

Besides, she was careful not to arouse suspicion. Each time, she waited politely for the men to catch up to her at the stables and once they were on their way, she made a point of not seeming to be anything but a clumsy rider.

At lunchtime that third day, she took the fresh grapes and nuts from her plate, along with the slices of bread that always accompanied her meal, and stashed them inside the deep pocket of the hooded robe Khalil had given her the day he'd taken her to Adaba.

'You ate well today, Joanna,' Rachelle said with a pleased smile, when she came to collect the lunch tray.

Joanna nodded. 'Everything was delicious. The grapes and nuts, especially, were wonderful!'

The girl's smile grew. 'I am glad you liked them. I shall make it a point to bring you more, for a snack.'

Joanna felt a twinge of guilt, but then she reminded herself that Rachelle, too, was her gaoler, the same as Khalil.

She smiled brightly. 'I'd like that.'

The snack went into the robe's pocket, too, along with the bread, cake, and raisins from dinner. It wasn't much, but it would have to do. She had no idea how long it would take her to reach the south, and freedom, but tomorrow she was going to make her break.

The next morning, well before breakfast, Joanna dressed, put on her hooded robe, then flung open her door. A guard she'd never before set eyes on stepped in front of her.

'Good morning,' she sang out and started past him.

The guard moved quickly into her path. He didn't have to speak. His body language said it all.

Joanna's heart pounded harder. 'Out of my way, please,' she said, dodging to the right. But he dodged, too, blocking the corridor. She faced him squarely, her back rigid with displeasure. 'I am going riding,' she said. When he didn't move, she repeated the words, more loudly and more slowly. 'I—am—going—riding. Do you hear me? Step aside, man!'

She thrust out her hand. It landed on his chest, a steel wall under the press of her palm, but he didn't move an inch. Joanna drew herself up.

'Get out of my way, you fool! I have the Prince's permission to ride. I'm going to the stables. Dammit, are you deaf?'

'What's the matter, Joanna?'

Joanna spun around. The child, Lilia, was standing behind her, her pretty face wearing a frown.

'Lilia.' Smiling, Joanna dropped to her knees and took the girl in her arms. 'How good to see you! I've missed you.'

Lilia smiled shyly. 'It is good to see you, too. I meant to ask Uncle Khalil if I might come to visit you, but he went away before I had the chance.' The little girl looked at the guard. 'Is Ali giving you trouble?'

It was hard not to laugh at the regal tone in the young voice. Joanna stood up, her hand on Lilia's shoulder, and nodded.

'Yes, he is. Your uncle gave permission for me to ride whenever I wished, but Ali doesn't seem aware of it.'

'Oh, you're just like me, Joanna,' Lilia said happily. 'I, too, like to ride just past dawn, when the earth smells sweet!' The girl stepped forward, a little figure accustomed to command. 'I will take care of Ali.'

Joanna held her breath while Lilia spoke. Ali's eyes darted to her. He didn't look happy, but, after a moment, he touched his hand to his forehead and stepped aside.

'Thank you,' Joanna said. Her knees felt weak with relief.

'May I ride with you?'

Joanna stared at the child. In her pleasure at seeing her, she'd all but forgotten her reason for this early morning ride. Now, guilt shot into her breast like a poisoned arrow.

'Oh, Lilia,' she said softly. 'I don't think——'

'Please?'

She glanced at the guard. The man was obviously uncertain of what to do next and suddenly she realised he'd yet to notify anyone that she was about to go riding.

Forgive me, Lilia, she thought.

'Yes, all right,' she said with a forced smile. She took the child's hand and they began walking, Lilia babbling

happily and the guard trailing uncertainly in the rear.
When they reached the stables, Lilia hesitated.

'I almost forgot,' she said. 'I may not ride without an
escort. I will tell Ali to send for——'

'No,' Joanna said quickly. She bit her lip, then
squatted down and framed the child's face in her hands.
'No,' she said softly, 'not yet. Why don't we have our
horses saddled first? That way, we'll be ready to ride
when the escort arrives.'

Lilia shrugged. 'As you wish, Joanna.'

The girl gave an order to the sleepy-eyed stable boy,
who led out the white mare and a roan pony. The pony
was saddled first, and then the boy turned to the mare.
But he'd only got the bridle on when the guard, who'd
grown increasingly restless, said something sharp-toned,
spun on his heel, and trotted out of the door.

There was no time to spare. Joanna bent quickly,
kissed Lilia's puzzled face.

'Forgive me, Lilia,' she whispered.

She straightened up, pushed the boy aside, and leaped
on Sidana's back. Quickly, she gathered up the reins and
kicked her heels hard into the mare's flanks. Before
anyone had time to move, the horse was out of the door
with Joanna bent low over its neck, riding hell-bent
for freedom.

CHAPTER ELEVEN

BY DUSK, Joanna was ready to admit what she'd known but refused to admit for hours. She was in trouble. She was hungry, thirsty, bone-weary from riding the mare without a saddle—and she was hopelessly, helplessly lost.

At first, she'd been so intent on making good her escape that she'd paid no attention to direction. All that had mattered was following the narrow dirt trail that led down the mountain to freedom.

She'd counted on the element of surprise to give her a decent head start and it had, at least five or six minutes. Eventually, though, she'd heard the pounding of hooves behind her. Glancing over her shoulder, she'd barely been able to make out the puffs of dust that marked the progress of the men riding after her. Even though she had the advantage, Joanna had known she could not outrun them for long.

Wildly, she'd glanced about, measuring her surroundings. There was a small copse of trees just off the trail. Desperate, she'd taken refuge in it only seconds before the riders had come thundering past. She'd been about to move out after them, seeing no choice but to play the risky game of following her followers, when she'd spied what had seemed to be a parallel path on the far side of the trees. Joanna had gritted her teeth and decided to go with the unknown.

For a while, her choice had seemed a good one. The path was narrower than the first and it twisted and turned like a snake, but it did lead down—only to suddenly peter out on the edge of a dizzying cliff.

A stone, dislodged by the mare's delicate hooves, ha
gone tumbling down into oblivion. Heart racing, Joann
had edged the animal away from the precipice but sł
hadn't gone all the way back up the trail for fear o
losing too much time. Instead, she'd cut through th
trees, pausing only long enough to dismount and rip th
telltale bells from the mare's bridle. Then she'd ridde
on until, at last, she'd come out in a narrow gorge.

Now, as the sun dropped a crimson mantle over th
surrounding mountain peaks, Joanna was trying 1
decide what to do next. She stared up at the sky. If th
setting sun were there, ahead of her, then east was d
rectly behind her, and north and south were—the
were...

A little sob of despair burst from her throat. Wha
did it matter? The points of the compass didn't mean
damn if you were trapped in a cage and didn't know th
way out.

An owl hooted mournfully in the trees. Joanna shuc
dered and burrowed more deeply into her jellaba. Tł
night was cool, and steadily growing cooler. The ma
was exhausted, head drooping, legs wobbly. She'd bee
wonderful and courageous, running like the wind afte
the first shock of being asked to do so, but for the pa
hour she'd moved at little more than a walk.

Except for the crescent moon hanging like a scimit.
over the trees, the darkness was complete. The owl's c
came again and just after it came another cry, that o
some small creature which had evidently met the ov
and lost the encounter.

Joanna shuddered again. She had to do somethin;
but what? Should she ride on, without any idea of whe
she was going? In the dark, the horse could easily mi
step; they'd both end up at the bottom of some abys

breakfast for the vultures she'd seen circling on the warm thermals of morning.

She could stop, give herself and her horse a rest. But if she did, she would lose whatever time she'd gained, perhaps give Khalil's men just the edge they needed to pick up her trail.

The mare lifted her head and snorted.

Joanna sat up straight, eyes wide as she peered into the darkness. Had the animal heard something?

Sidana snorted again and pawed the ground with a hoof. Joanna bent over her neck, patted it soothingly.

'What is it?' she whispered. 'Is there something out there?'

The horse took a tentative step forward. Joanna hesitated, and then she loosened her hold on the reins and gave the animal its head. Wherever the mare was leading had to be better than this.

Sidana's pace quickened. She was almost trotting now, and all at once Joanna understood. Ahead, just visible in the pale wash of moonlight, a spring bubbled from a rocky cairn and trickled into the trough-shaped depression it had worn into the rock over the centuries.

Joanna smiled. 'Good girl!'

She slid carefully to the ground, groaning. Muscles she hadn't known existed ached. She had not ridden bareback since a childhood summer spent on a Montana mining property.

The mare buried her nose in the shallow water and Joanna squatted beside her, sipping from her cupped hands, not caring that she and the horse were sharing their drink. Thirst had become a growing discomfort; she'd known it might be, but how could she have stolen a Thermos of fruit juice from her meal tray without drawing Rachelle's attention?

The horse, replete, lifted her head and whinnied softly.

'It does taste good, doesn't it?' Joanna murmured.
'I'm glad I gave you your head, girl, otherwise——'

What was that? Joanna stiffened. She could hear
something. Voices. Male voices, low-pitched but carrying clearly on the still air, and now the sound of hooves
and the creak of leather.

Khalil's men! They'd picked up her trail! Joanna
snatched up the mare's trailing reins and led her back
into the trees.

'Shh,' she whispered frantically, holding the animal'
bridle with one hand and stroking its nose with the other
'shh!'

She couldn't let them find her now, not after she'
come so far. Even if it took her until dawn to find th
path that would lead her down the mountain, she wasn'
going back, she couldn't go back, she——

There! She could see them now. They were headin
for the spring. A dozen men, not any more than that-
but—but——

But who were they? Surely, not Khalil's followers. Sh
had never seen their faces before, and their clothing wa
all wrong.

The men dismounted, all but one obscenely fat ma
who she knew instinctively must be their leader and wh
barked out commands. One man scurried to the sprin
dipped a cup into the water, hurried back and offere
it with downcast eyes. The fat man drank thirstily, tosse
the cup into the dirt, and slid clumsily from the sadd
to the ground.

Joanna's gaze flew over the other men. They we
heavily armed and had a grim, ugly look to them. A
you didn't have to understand their words to shudder
their tone of voice.

The fat man snarled another command and one of th
men bowed and answered. His answer meant nothing

oanna, except for the last words and the fearful respect
hat laced them.

'...Abu Al Zouad.'

Joanna's breath caught. Of course! The fat man was
Abu Al Zouad! Her father had described him to her.
Abu was a big man, he'd said, grossly overweight and
lumsy, given to expensive Italian suits and too much
old jewellery.

What would he say now, if he saw him dressed in a
reasy jellaba, his chest bristling with bandoliers of
mmunition?

The men were clustered in little knots, smoking ciga-
ettes and murmuring quietly to each other. Abu clapped
is hands and they looked up as he began to speak. It
as a long speech, and again incomprehensible to
oanna, except for two simple words that were repeated
ver and over.

Joanna Bennett.

Abu was talking about her! Had he come to free her?
his looked more like a raiding party than a rescue
iission, but Joanna wasn't a child. It wasn't only the
ood guys who wore white hats.

But why would her father authorise a risky attempt
t rescue instead of negotiating for her freedom? Joanna
lew out her breath. Perhaps—perhaps Khalil had not
old her the truth? For all she knew, Sam might have
iade every possible effort to gain her release, only to
e rebuffed by Khalil. In desperation, he might surely
nd men to find and free her.

It was reasonable, even logical—but if it were, what
as keeping her from stepping out into the clearing and
elling, hey, here I am, Abu? Why was she still hiding,
ill praying that her horse would not suddenly whinny
nd give away her position?

Abu finished speaking. One of his men said some
thing; she heard her name fall from his lips, and th
others chuckled. Abu shook his head and pointed t
himself, and their laughter grew.

There was something in the sound of the laughter, i
the way her name had been used and in the way Ab
had stabbed that pudgy finger at himself, that sent
chill along Joanna's spine.

She swallowed hard. The men were mounting up. I
another moment, they'd ride out of here and she'd b
alone again, and just as lost as she'd been before the
arrived.

Now was the time to step forward, to call out Abu'
name and identify herself. Determinedly, before sh
could lose courage, Joanna began rising slowly from he
crouched position——

A hand clamped over her mouth and an arm, powerfu
and hard as steel, closed around her. Joanna cried ou
soundlessly and began to struggle, but she was helples
against the strength of the man holding her.

'Joanna!' Khalil's voice whispered into her ear. 'Sto
it, Joanna! It's me.'

She almost sobbed with relief. She went still, an
Khalil lowered her slowly to the ground, his arm r
maining around her waist.

'You mustn't make a sound,' he said softly. 'Do yo
understand?'

She nodded and he took his hand from her lip
Beyond the trees, the little group of riders was just va
ishing into the night.

She swung around and looked at Khalil. In the moo
light, she could see that he was unshaven, that there w:
a grim set to his mouth and that lines of weariness fanne
out from his eyes, and yet she had never seen a man s
beautiful. She had escaped his silken prison, she thougl

with a sudden catch in her breath, but how would she ever escape the memory of him?

The realisation was as stunning as it was bewildering. She whispered his name, but he shook his head, the stony expression on his face unchanging.

'There will be time for talk later.'

Najib stood just behind his master, ears pricked forward. Khalil took the animal's reins and set off through the trees, in the opposite direction from the spring with Joanna and her mare following after him.

A ten-minute walk brought them to what looked like a labyrinth of giant boulders and, at its end, the yawning, dark mouth of a cave.

Khalil tethered the horses in a blind passageway among the boulders, where no casual observer would see them, and then he took Joanna's hand and led her through the maze up into the cave.

'I played here often, as a boy,' he said, his voice echoing off the stone walls. 'It's deep enough for safety, and there's even a narrow cleft in the rocks at the cave's end that we can use to get out, if we should have to.'

Within minutes, he'd swept together a small pile of kindling and brush and lit a fire deep in the cave's interior. Joanna held her breath as he turned towards her. They had been alone before, but this time was different. She had been running away from him, it was true, but now, seeing him again, being so close to him, she felt— she felt——

'What the hell did you think you were doing?'

She blinked. Khalil's face was taut with barely contained fury.

'I don't—I don't know what you mean.'

'I don't know what you mean,' he mimicked. His mouth tightened. 'For a woman who always has a clever answer at her fingertips, that one is pathetic!'

Her spine stiffened. 'It is not!'

'If you behave like a fool, I'll treat you like one.'

She stared at him for a moment, and then she whirled around and started towards the mouth of the cave. His hand fell on her shoulder.

'Where do you think you're going?' he growled.

'Where I should have gone in the first place. With Abu. If you hadn't come along and ruined things——'

Khalil spun her towards him. 'You gave me your word, Joanna! But I should have known that such a simple pledge was beyond you.'

'What are you talking about?'

'You promised you would not ride alone!'

Joanna tossed her head. 'But I didn't promise I'd willingly remain your prisoner.'

'You little idiot! I'm not talking about escape. I'm talking about danger.'

'The danger of disobeying the rules of a petty dictator, you mean!'

'It is dangerous for anyone, but especially for a woman, to ride these mountains alone.'

'You never said that.'

'I didn't think I had to,' he said, glowering at her. 'Anyone with half a brain——'

'Stop it! I'm tired of your insults!'

'Then don't set yourself up for them. If you'd used your head, you'd have realised I gave you those instructions to keep you safe.'

'Oh, yes.' Joanna's voice shook, and she could feel the sting of tears in her eyes, although there was no reason to want to cry. 'Yes, you'd want me kept safe, wouldn't you? If I were hurt or damaged, what sort of bargaining chip would I be?'

His eyes narrowed. 'Bargaining chip?'

'What's the matter? Isn't your English good enough
understand a simple phrase? A bargaining chip is what
hostage is. It's——'

She cried out as he swept her into his arms and kissed
er, his mouth taking hers with a passion so urgent it
ole her breath away, and then he clasped her face in
s hands and drew back just enough so he could look
to her eyes.

'You cannot be so blind,' he whispered. 'Surely you
e that you have become much more than my hostage.'

'No,' she said shakily, 'no, I don't see.'

He smiled, and suddenly his eyes were tender. 'Let me
ow you, then,' he said softly, and slowly, his head de-
ended to hers.

He kissed her gently, his mouth moving softly against
ers, his hands spreading under the hood and into her
air. A tremor went through her, but she didn't respond.

'Joanna,' he said, his lips still clinging to hers,
oanna, Joanna...'

And suddenly a wave of emotion, as unexpected and
fierce as a tidal wave, swept through her. She began
tremble.

'Khalil?' she whispered, and the question inherent in
e single word was enough. He caught her in his arms
d kissed her insistently. Her lips parted beneath his,
er arms stole around his neck, and she clung to him
d knew she would never, not in a thousand lifetimes,
ant to let him go.

'How did you find me?' she sighed, while he pressed
tle kisses to her temples and eyelids. 'And where did
ou come from? You were gone——'

'I was drawn away deliberately by Abu. It was a clever
heme, but there are few secrets that can be kept in this
art of the world. I turned back when the information

reached me, contacted my men, told them to put yo
under armed guard.'

'Abu was coming to free me, then?'

Khalil hesitated. 'It might be better to say that yo
were all the excuse he needed to ride against me.'

'But—what will happen when he reaches your villag
Will your people be safe?'

He smiled grimly. 'He's riding into a trap. My me
are waiting for him.'

'But how...?'

'Joanna.' He stroked the hair back from her face. '
don't want to talk about Abu now,' he whispered.

His mouth took hers again, this time in a deeper, mo
passionate kiss. Joanna moaned softly, and he lowere
his head and put his mouth to her throat, as if to measur
the racing pulse beating in its hollow.

She whispered his name as he eased the jellaba fro
her shoulders. His eyes burned into hers as he undid th
buttons of her shirt. When it fell away, he drew bac
and looked at her with such hunger that she felt he
breasts lift and harden under his gaze.

'You are so beautiful.' He reached out slowly an
stroked his fingers across her nipples. 'You are mor
beautiful than any woman I have ever seen.'

'You're beautiful, too,' she whispered. The skin tigh
ened across his cheekbones as she slid his jellaba fro
his shoulders. Her fingers trembled as she undid th
buttons on his shirt. She slid her hands under the so
cotton, exulting in the feel of his silken skin, his ta
muscles, and in the hiss of his breath when she touche
him.

He caught her hand in his, carried it to his lips an
pressed a kiss into her palm.

'I want to see all of you, Joanna.'

She stood still as he stripped away her shoes, her ousers, and, finally, her panties. Colour raced up under er skin as she watched him look at her, not from emarrassment but from the sweet pain of wanting him. Ier body was already damp, ready for his, and although e had barely touched her so far, her blood was at a ever pitch.

'Now you,' she whispered.

She lifted her eyes to his as she reached out to his belt uckle. He made a sound in the back of his throat as he opened it. She swept her hand lightly down the length f his fly, her breath catching when she felt his arousal. Iis fingers curled around her wrist and he smiled tightly.

'Be careful,' he said. 'If you go on playing this game, he night may end before it begins.'

A smile curved across Joanna's mouth. 'Am I to obey ou, my lord?'

He laughed as he caught her up in his arms, snatched p Najib's saddle blanket, and walked deeper into the ave, to where the fire's glow was only a soft reflection.

'We will obey each other on this night, my beloved.'

Slowly, he eased her down on the blanket, laid her ack, and bent over her, his face shadowed and myserious in the firelight.

'I wanted you from the moment I saw you,' he whispered.

Joanna laughed throatily. 'I thought you wanted to hrottle me from the moment you saw me.'

Khalil chuckled. 'You are right. There have been times I didn't know which I wanted to do more.' His smile faded as he looked at her. 'But tonight—tonight,' he whispered, 'there is only one thing I wish to do tonight.'

He touched her with his fingertips, slowly following the curve of breast and belly, then moving lightly against her thighs. She whispered his name, held out her arms to him, but he ignored her, bending over her body so that he could trace the same path again, this time with his mouth. She moaned softly as his lips closed first on one breast, then on the other. When he drew back and bent again to kiss her thighs, her voice rose quavering into the silence of the cave. And when, finally, his mouth closed on the sweet centre of her, Joanna cried out his name in ecstasy.

The stars were still tumbling from the sky when he rose over her.

'Look at me,' he said. Joanna opened her eyes and he smiled down at her, a sweet, fierce smile of possession and dominance that made her heart seem to stop—but when he entered her, slowly, so slowly, with his eyes never leaving hers, she knew that her possession of him, her dominance of him, was as complete as his was of her.

She loved him, she adored him, and it stunned her that it had taken her so long to recognise the truth.

She wanted to tell him that, to whisper that he was the captor not of her body but of her heart and of her soul, but he was deep within her now and she was, oh, she was——

'Beloved,' he said fiercely, and kissed her deeply. Joanna cried out as she spun into the night sky, where she became a burst of quicksilver among the stars.

Joanna awoke once, during the night, drawn from sleep by the sweet touch of Khalil's mouth. Her awakening was slow and dreamlike, and after they'd made love she settled into his arms and fell back into deep sleep.

But when she awoke again, she was alert, uncertain as to what it was that had roused her. She lay very still, tension building in her muscles, and then she heard the faint whicker of a horse and she sighed with relief.

That was what had awakened her, the mare or Najib, offering gentle protests at having spent the night tethered.

Joanna smiled. She, too, had spent the night tethered, held closely in Khalil's arms—and it had been the most wonderful night of her life. She turned her face against his shoulder, inhaling the clean, masculine smell of his body, touching her lips lightly to his satiny skin, and gazed at his face.

How different he looked in sleep. The little lines that fanned out from his eyes were almost invisible, his mouth was soft, as if, in sleep, he could put aside, at least for a while, the burden of leadership he carried. She sighed and put her head against his chest, listening to the steady beat of his heart. And that burden had to be even heavier, knowing that part of his country had been stolen from him, that it was in the grip of an evil despot, for Joanna no longer had any doubts at all about Abu Al Zouad.

Her father had been wrong, whether through accident or design. Khalil was not the bandit. Abu was, and the sooner she was able to tell Sam that she knew the truth now, the better.

There it was, that sound again. Joanna sat up, tossing her hair back from her face. She was sure it was one of the horses, but what if the animal was whinnying a warning instead of protesting against inactivity?

She dropped a gentle kiss on Khalil's forehead, then rose to her feet, found her clothing, and dressed. It had been hard to see much last night, but she remembered that the cave entrance was on a slight elevation. Quietly, she made her way forward. Perhaps she could see what it was that——

A hand whipped across her mouth. Joanna gasped, kicked out sharply, and other hands caught hold of her and dragged her into the sunlight, where Abu and the rest of his men waited.

'Good morning, Miss Bennett.' Joanna glared at the fat man as he slid from his horse. He strolled towards her, smiling unpleasantly. 'I am His Excellency, Abu Al Zouad.' His smile became a grin, revealing a shiny, gold tooth. 'You don't look very happy to see me.'

Joanna's mind was spinning. Abu wasn't bothering to drop his voice. And now that she'd appeared, no one was paying any attention to the cave.

They had no idea Khalil was with her! He could escape through the rear of the cave. All she had to do was be certain he heard this fuss and awakened.

She bit down hard on the hand that covered her mouth. The man cursed, let her go, and lifted his hand to strike her.

'I wouldn't do that,' she said in her best Bennett voice. Whether he understood her English or not, her tone stopped him. He glanced at Abu, who motioned him away.

'Well, Miss Bennett. It is good to see that captivity has not dulled your spirit.'

Joanna's chin lifted. 'How did you find me?'

Abu smiled. 'My spies alerted me to your rather abrupt departure from the fortress of the bandit Khalil, and then it was simply a matter of following your trail— although I must admit, my scout stumbled upon your little hideaway quite by accident.' He moved closer to her. 'And now I have my prize.' Without warning, he reached out and ran his hand down her body. 'And what a prize it is, too!'

Joanna's blood went cold. She thought of Khalil's hesitation last night, when she'd asked him if Abu were coming to rescue her.

'It might be better to say that you were all the excuse he needed to ride against me,' he'd said.

Abu had no intention of taking her back to her father! He would kill her—after first taking his pleasure—and blame her death on Khalil.

Joanna slapped his hand away. 'I am not your prize!' The man nearest Abu snarled something and put his hand on the scabbard hanging from his belt. 'You have forgotten who I am,' she said, her voice so sharp and chill that only she knew she was really trembling with fear.

'I forget nothing,' Abu growled. 'You are a woman, stolen by a bandit. Whatever happens to you will be his doing, not mine.'

'And losing the reward for my return will be your doing—or are you so rich you can't use a million dollars in gold?'

'A million dollars? Your father did not say——'

Joanna drew herself fully erect. 'A million dollars, and the contract you want so badly with Bennettco. You will get neither, if I am not returned safely.'

'You are only a woman! You make no rules for Sam Bennett.'

'I am his daughter.'

'That is a guarantee of nothing.'

Joanna smiled tightly. 'Perhaps—and perhaps not.' With a last bit of bravado, she looked him straight in the eye. 'Are you willing to take that chance?'

She could almost see the wheels spinning in his ugly head, but her most desperate thoughts were deep within the cave. Had Khalil got away? Had he heard the noise, made good his escape? Had he——?

Her answer came in a sudden burst of sound, a bloodchilling yell that froze her with terror. It must have had the same effect on Abu's men, too, for when Khalil came bursting from the cave entrance there was time for him to lunge at Abu and almost curl his hands around the man's throat before anyone moved.

'Go on,' he yelled at Joanna as two men pulled him back and pinned him against the rocks, 'make a run for it! Dammit, woman, why are you standing there?'

Abu rubbed his dirty fingers over his throat. 'Well, well,' he said, very softly, 'this is indeed a morning of prizes—and of surprises.' He grinned, then pointed at one of his men. 'Kill the bandit!'

'No!' The word ripped from Joanna's throat. She stepped forward. 'No,' she said again, 'don't kill him.'

'We will spare you,' Abu said, as if it were an act of humanity that impelled him and not the threat Joanna had made. 'But I have waited too long for a reason the people will accept to kill the bandit.' He smiled. 'And now I have one. Kill him!'

'Very well.' Joanna's voice was cool. 'Kill him, if you like—but if you do, you are a fool.'

'Watch your tongue, woman!'

'He is not only your enemy, Abu, he is also my father's. He has dishonoured him—and me.' She took a breath. 'My father will surely want the pleasure of killing Khalil himself.'

Abu laughed. 'Westerners do not believe in taking blood for dishonour.'

'Do you think my father got where he is today by being soft-hearted?'

She looked over at Khalil, expecting to see a dark glint of admiration for her off-the-cuff cleverness in his eyes, needing to see it to give her the courage to go on. Her heart dropped like a stone. Khalil was watching her as if she were something that had just scurried out from under a rock. She turned away quickly, forcing herself to concentrate on Abu.

'My father will pay for having Khalil delivered into his hands,' she said coldly, 'and he will be grateful to you forever.'

'I think you say this to save the neck of the man who has become your lover.'

Joanna stared at him. 'No. No, I——'

'I think I am right, Miss Bennett.' He looked at one of the men holding Khalil. 'Go on,' he said, 'kill him!'

'He took me,' Joanna blurted. 'He forced me! That's why I made such a desperate escape.' She knotted her hands into fists, marched up to Khalil and looked into his eyes, which were almost black with rage. My love, she thought, oh, my love!

Swiftly, before she lost courage, she drew saliva into her mouth and spat full into Khalil's face.

'He's a barbarian,' she said, swinging away so she didn't have to look at him, 'and I'll have no peace until my father takes my revenge.'

A heavy silence descended on the group, broken only by the laboured sound of Khalil's breathing, and then Abu nodded.

'Very well. We take him with us and——'

Cries filled the air. Joanna shrank back as Khalil's men came riding up the slope. Within minutes, it was over. Abu and his men were defeated.

With a little sob of joy, Joanna ran to Khalil and threw her arms around him, but he shoved her away.

'Don't touch me,' he said in a soft, dangerous whisper.

'Khalil. My love! I was bargaining for your life! Surely you didn't believe——'

'And now you are bargaining for your own!' He stepped forward, grasping her arms and yanking her close. 'Be grateful I am not the savage you think I am,' he growled. 'If I were, I would gladly slit your throat and leave you here for the vultures.' He flung her from him and strode to Najib, who stood waiting beside the white mare. 'Take her to the airstrip,' he snapped to one of his men, 'and have her flown to Casablanca. We have

Abu—Sam Bennett can have his daughter.' He leaped on to Najib's back, grasped the reins, and gave Joanna one last, terrible look. 'They deserve each other.'

He dug his heels hard into Najib's flanks. The horse rose on its hind legs, pawed the air, then spun away with its rider sitting proudly in the saddle.

It was the last Joanna saw of Khalil.

CHAPTER TWELVE

THE doorman pushed open the door and smiled as Joanna stepped from her taxi and made her way towards him.

'Evening, Miss Bennett,' he said. 'Hot enough to fry eggs on the pavement, isn't it?'

Joanna smiled back at him. 'Hello, Rogers. Yes, but New York in August is always pretty awful.'

The lift operator smiled, too, and offered a similar comment on the weather as the car rose to the twelfth floor, and Joanna said something clever in return, as she was expected to do.

It was a relief to stop all the smiling and stab her key into the lock of her apartment door. Smiling was the last thing she felt like doing lately. With a weary sigh, she stepped out of her high heels and dropped her handbag on a table in the foyer.

Sam kept saying she'd developed all the charm of a woman sucking on a lemon, and she supposed it was true—but in the three months she'd been back from Casablanca she hadn't found all that much to smile about.

Joanna popped off her earrings as she made her way towards her bedroom. She was vice-president of Bennettco now, she had an office of her own, a staff, and even her father's grudging respect.

So why wasn't it enough? she thought as she peeled off her dress and underthings.

She stepped into the blue tiled bathroom and turned on the shower. The water felt delicious but she couldn't

171

luxuriate beneath it for long. In less than an hour, Sam was picking her up. They were going to another of the endless charity affairs he insisted they attend, this time at the Palace Hotel.

A mirthless smile angled across her lips as she stepped from the shower and towelled herself dry. The Palace. She had been to it before, knew that it dripped crystal chandeliers and carpeting deep enough to cushion the most delicate foot. But she remembered a real palace, one that boasted no such touches of elegance, yet had been more a palace than the hotel would ever be.

Damn, but she wished she hadn't seen that little squib in the paper at breakfast! 'Jandaran Prince Consolidates Hold on Kingdom, Seeks Financing for Mining Project', it had said, and she'd shoved the paper away without reading further, but it had been enough. A rush of memories had spoiled the day, although she couldn't imagine why. She didn't care what happened to Khalil. She had never loved him. How could she have, when they came from such different worlds? It was just that she'd been frightened, and despairing, and there was no point pretending he wasn't a handsome, virile male.

An image flashed into her mind as she reached for her mascara. She saw Khalil leaning over her, his eyes dark with desire. Joanna, he was whispering, Joanna, my beloved...

Her hand slipped and a dark smudge bloomed on her cheek. She wiped it off, then bent towards the mirror again and painted a smile on her lips. What had happened in Jandara was a closed chapter. No one even knew about her part in it, thanks to Sam.

'I didn't tell a soul,' he'd said, after she'd finally reached Casablanca.

'Not even the State Department?' she'd asked, remembering shadowy fragments of something Khalil had said the night he'd abducted her.

'Not even them. I was afraid I might compromise your safety. How could I know what an animal like Khalil might do if I called out the troops? That's why I couldn't give in to his demands. I figured once I did, the bastard might kill you. You understand, don't you?'

Joanna had assured him that she did. Sam hadn't been saying anything she hadn't thought of herself. Sending Abu after her had been the only way he'd thought he could rescue her. As for Abu—Sam had been duped, he'd said with feeling.

'The guy had me fooled. How could I have known what he really was like?'

Joanna slid open the wardrobe in her bedroom and took a sequinned blue gown from its hanger. The only fly in the ointment was that the proposed mining deal had gone down the tubes. Khalil had wasted no time making sure of that. Within twelve hours, Abu had been sentenced to life imprisonment, Khalil had been restored to the throne of Jandara, and the Bennett contract had been returned by messenger, accompanied by a terse note, signed by Khalil.

'We will develop the property ourselves.'

Sam had turned red with anger and cursed and then said hell, win some, lose some, what did it matter? He had his Jo back. That was all that counted.

Joanna whisked a brush through her hair. He was right. That was what counted, that she was back, and if sometimes, at night, she awoke from dreams she could not remember with tears on her cheeks, so what? She was getting ahead rapidly at Bennettco and that was what she wanted. It was all she wanted.

She glanced at the clock. It was time. Quickly she stuffed a comb, tissues and her lipstick into an evening bag, slipped on a pair of glittery high-heeled sandals, and made her way out of the door.

Sam was waiting at the kerb in his chauffeured Lincoln. 'Hello, babe,' he said when she stepped inside. 'Mmm, you look delicious.'

Joanna's eyebrows rose. 'What gives?'

He chuckled as the car eased into traffic. 'What do you mean, what gives? Can't I give my girl a compliment?'

'You're as transparent as glass, Father,' she said with a wry smile. 'Whenever you want something from me and you expect a refusal, you begin laying on compliments.'

He sat back and sighed. 'I was just thinking, on the way over here, what a terrible time that bastard put us through.'

Joanna's smile faded. 'Khalil?'

He smiled coldly. 'What other bastard do we know? To think he locked you up, treated you like dirt——'

'I really don't want to talk about him tonight, Father.'

'Did you know he's in town?'

She shrugged, trying for a casual tone. 'Is he?'

Sam grunted. 'Abu may have been a brute,' he said, 'but Khalil's no better.'

Joanna looked at him. 'You know that's not true!'

'You're not defending him, are you, Jo?'

Was she? Joanna shook her head. 'No,' she said quickly, 'of course not.'

'It burns my butt that the man treated you the way he did and gets rewarded for it,' Sam said testily. 'There he is, sitting in Abu's palace, snug as a quail in tall grass, counting up the coins in the national treasury.'

Joanna closed her eyes wearily. 'I doubt that.'

Sam chuckled. 'But we'll have the last laugh, kid. I've seen to that.'

Joanna turned towards her father. There was something in his tone that was unsettling.

'What do you mean?'

'We may have lost the mining deal—but so has Khalil!'

'He's not. He's going to put together a consortium himself.'

'He's going to try and milk a fat profit straight into his own pockets, you mean.'

'No,' Joanna said quickly. 'He'd never——'

'How do you think he'll like having the world hear he wanted the fortune tucked away in those mountains so badly he killed for it?' Sam said, his eyes glittering.

Joanna stared at her father. 'Killed who?'

'Abu. Who else?'

'But Khalil didn't kill him. He's in prison. And it isn't because of the fortune in those mountains, it's——'

'For God's sake, Jo!' Sam's voice lost its cheerful edge and took on a rapier sharpness. 'Who cares what the facts are? I'm telling you I've come up with a way to put a knife in that s.o.b.'s back for what he did to us!'

'Us? *Us*? He didn't do anything to us. I was the one he took, the one whose——'

'What? What were you going to say?'

She stared at him in bewilderment. She knew what she'd been going to say, that she was the one whose heart was broken. But it wasn't true. She was defending Khalil, yes, but not because she loved him. It was only because it would be wrong to lie about him, to raise doubts in the minds of his people.

'You can't do something so evil,' she said flatly.

Sam's face hardened. 'Listen to me, Joanna. Khalil's trying to put together this mining deal, sure. But when the banks and the power brokers know the truth about

him, how he abducted you and how he treated
you——'

'But they won't.' Joanna's eyes flashed with defiance.
'The story's mine, and I'm not going to tell it.'

Sam's mouth thinned with distaste. 'It's useless,
treating you as if you understood business! You're not
the son I wanted, and you never will be.'

Tears glinted on Joanna's lashes. 'Well,' she said, 'at
least it's finally out in the open. I'm not, no, and——'

The car jounced to a stop at the kerb. Joanna grabbed
her evening bag from the seat. 'We can discuss this later,
Father.'

'Jo. Wait!'

She snatched her hand from his and reached for the
door, too angry and upset to wait for the chauffeur to
open it. Sam cared about protocol, but it had never
meant a damn to her.

'Joanna,' Sam said sharply, but she ignored him,
swung open the door—and stepped straight into a bewildering sea of cameras and microphones.

'Miss Bennett!' Someone shoved a mike into her face.
'Is it true,' an eager voice asked, 'that you were abducted and held for ransom by the new ruler of Jandara?'

Joanna stiffened. 'Where did you——?'

'Is it true he abducted you because he'd demanded
bribe money from your father's company and your father
refused to pay it?'

She spun towards Sam, who had stepped out of the
car after her. 'Did you do this?' she said in a low voice.

His eyes narrowed. 'We'll discuss this later, you said.
I think we should stay with that idea.'

'Answer me! Did you set this up?'

'Do unto others as they do unto you, Jo,' Sam said
out of the side of his mouth. 'Khalil's in New York, his
hat in his hand. It's my turn now.'

Joanna's mouth trembled. 'You would lie about Khalil, let the media swarm over me, all to get even?'

Sam glared at her. 'Business is business, Joanna. How come you can't get that straight?' He pushed past her, making it look as if he were defending her against the press, and held up his hands. 'My daughter finds this too emotional a topic to talk about,' he said. 'I'll speak on her behalf.'

He launched into a tirade against Khalil, about his greed and his barbarism, about how he'd been angered by Bennettco's refusal to pay enough *baksheesh* and how he'd stolen Joanna in retaliation, then demanded a king's ransom for her return——

'No,' Joanna said.

The microphones and cameras swung towards her and Sam did too, his eyes stabbing her with a warning look.

'The only reason we've decided to come forward now,' he said, 'is because my daughter refuses to let Prince Khalil trick our bankers into investing in——'

'No!' Joanna's voice rose. 'It's not true!'

'Do you see what the bastard did?' Sam roared. 'She's still afraid to talk about how he imprisoned her, starved her, beat her——'

'It's a lie!' Joanna stepped past her father. 'Prince Khalil asked for no ransom, no bribes. He's a good, decent man, and my father's trying to blacken his name!'

There was a moment's silence, and then a voice rang out.

'Decent men don't abduct women.'

There was a titter of laughter. Joanna lifted her chin and stared directly into the glittering eyes of the video cameras.

'He didn't abduct me,' she said in a clear voice.

'Your father says he did. What's the story, Miss Bennett?'

What had Khalil said, the night he'd taken her? Tha
he could tell the world she'd run off with him and b
believed, that no one would doubt such a story. Joanna
took a deep breath.

'I was with Khalil because I wanted to be with him,
she said. She heard her father growl a short, ugly word
and her voice gathered strength. 'The Prince asked m
to go away with him—and I did.'

A dozen questions filled the air, and finally one re
porter's voice cut through the rest.

'So, you don't hate the Hawk of the North?'

Joanna's lips trembled. 'No,' she said, 'I don't hat
him.'

'What, then?' someone called.

Joanna hesitated. 'I—I——'

'Well, Miss Bennett?' another voice insisted, 'how d
you feel about him?'

Joanna stared at the assembled cameras. How did sh
feel about Khalil? What did she feel?

A woman reporter jostled aggressively past the other
and stuck a microphone under her nose.

'Do you love him?' she said, her crimson lips partin
in a smirk.

Joanna looked at the woman. The time for lies an
deceit was past.

'Yes,' she whispered, 'I do.'

She heard Sam's groan, heard the babble of voices a
trying to question her at once, and then she turned an
fled into a taxi that had mercifully just disgorged i
passengers.

Joanna stalked the length of the terrace that opened o
her living-room. The night had proven even warmer tha
the afternoon; the long, white silk robe she wore wa

tight against her skin but even so, she felt as if she were smothering.

But she knew it had little to do with the temperature. She was smothering of humiliation, and there was nothing she could do about it.

She groaned out loud and sank down on the edge of a *chaise longue*. How could she have made such an ass of herself?

I love him, she'd said—but she didn't. She *didn't* love Khalil, she never had.

So why had she said such a preposterous thing? Anger at Sam, yes, and pain at how he'd been prepared to use her, but still, why would she have made such an announcement?

She rose and walked slowly into the living-room, just as the clock on the mantel chimed the hour. Four a.m. If only it were dawn, she'd put on her running shoes, a T-shirt and shorts, and go for a long run through Central Park. Maybe that would help. Maybe——

The phone shrilled, as it had periodically through the night. Would it be the Press, which had found her despite her ex-directory listing, or Sam, who'd called three times to tell her she had ruined him? She snatched it up and barked a hello.

It was Sam, but the tone of his voice told her that his rage had given way to weariness.

'Will you at least apologise for making fools of me and of Bennettco, Jo?'

Joanna put a hand to her forehead. 'Of course. I never intended to embarrass you, Father.'

'How could you do it, then? My reputation and the company's are in shambles.'

She smiled. 'You've survived worse.'

Sam sighed gustily into the phone. 'I'm not saying you were right,' he said, 'but maybe my idea wasn't so hot.'

Joanna's smile broadened. 'Are *you* apologising to *me*, Father?'

'I've always walked a thin line between what's right and what's wrong and sometimes—sometimes, I lose my way.'

It was an admission she would never have expected and it touched her.

'You're one tough lady, Joanna,' Sam said quietly.

'I love you, Father,' Joanna whispered.

'And I love you.' She heard him take a deep breath. 'Jo? I really did believe I'd endanger you by negotiating with Khalil. That's the only reason I didn't tear up that blasted contract. I want to be sure you know that. You mean the world to me.'

Tears stung her eyes. 'I know.'

'Well,' Sam said brusquely, 'it's late. You should get some sleep.' There was a silence. 'Goodnight, daughter.'

Daughter. He had never called her that before. Joanna's hand tightened on the phone.

'Goodnight, Daddy,' she said.

She hung up the phone and smiled. So, she thought, stretching her legs out in front of her, some good had come of this mess after all. She and her father might yet be friends——

She started as the doorbell rang. Who could it be, at this late hour? Who could the doorman have possibly admitted without calling her on the intercom first?

Joanna stood and walked slowly to the door. A reporter, she thought grimly, a reporter who'd sneaked in the back way.

The bell rang again, the sound persistent and jarring in the middle of the night silence.

'Go away,' she called.

Someone rapped sharply at the door.

'Do you hear me? If you don't get away from here his minute, I'll call the police!'

'You call them,' a man's voice growled, 'or your eighbours will, when I break this door down!'

Joanna fell back against the wall. 'Khalil?' she whispered.

'Do you hear me, Joanna? Open this door at once!'

'No,' she said, staring at the door as if it might fly ff its hinges. 'Go away!'

'Very well, Joanna. We'll wait for someone to phone he police. They'll probably show up with a dozen reporters in tow, but that's fine with me. Jandara can use ll the publicity it can get.'

She flew at the door, her fingers trembling as they ced across the locks, and then she threw the door open. 'How dare you do this?'

'This is America,' Khalil said with a cold smile. 'People an do anything they want in America. Didn't you tell e that once?'

'No! I certainly did not. I——'

Joanna fell silent. Khalil was dressed much as he had en the night they'd met, in a dark suit and white shirt, ut somewhere along the way, he'd taken off his tie, ndone the top buttons of his shirt, and slung his jacket ver his shoulder. He looked handsome and wonderful, d the sight of him made her feel giddy.

She clutched her silk robe to her throat. 'You can't me in!'

He smiled, showing even, white teeth. 'Can't I?'

'No. This is my apartment, and——' The door ammed shut behind him as he pushed past her into the yer. 'Damn you,' Joanna cried. 'Didn't you hear what said? I don't want you here. Get out!'

Khalil shook his head. 'No.'

No. Just that one word, delivered in that insolent, imperious voice...

Joanna tossed her head. 'All right, then, wait here and get thrown out! The doorman's probably on the phone this very minute, calling the——'

'The doorman,' he said with a smug little smile, 'is chatting with my minister.' He folded his arms over his chest in that impossibly arrogant manner she detested. 'Did you know the man was born a stone's throw from Hassan's birthplace?'

Joanna's eyes narrowed. 'Hassan was born in Brooklyn?'

Khalil grinned. 'Well, perhaps he stretched things a bit. But it is true that Hassan has a cousin who was born in Brooklyn.'

Joanna lifted her chin in defiance. 'As far as I'm concerned, you and Hassan could have a string of cousins who——'

'We were at a dinner party all this evening, Joanna.'

'Isn't that wonderful,' she said sweetly. 'I'm delighted for you both.'

'I only just got back to my hotel, and I turned on—what do you call it?—the twenty-four-hour-a-day news channel——'

'I am certain there are lots of people who'd be interested in a minute-by-minute accounting of how you spent your evening, Khalil, but personally——'

'I saw your news conference.'

Joanna felt her face go white. 'What news conference?' she said with false bravado. 'I don't know what you're talking about.'

'That informative little gathering you arranged outside the Palace Hotel.' A cool smile curved over his lips. 'That news conference.'

'It wasn't a news conference, it was a circus. Now, if
ou're quite finished——'

'What a clever pair you and your father are, Joanna.'
She gaped at him. 'What?'

'Telling two such disparate but fascinating stories to
ιe Press.' Khalil's eyes narrowed. 'What better way for
ennettco to garner publicity, hmm?'

'What better way for...' Joanna burst out laughing.
s that what you think? That Sam and I set that up?'

'Didn't you?'

'No, of course not. What would be the point?'

'How do I know? Perhaps the price of Bennettco's
ock has fallen and you two decided front-page head-
nes would shore it up.'

Joanna shook her head in disbelief. 'My father would
e proud of you, thinking of something like that.'

'You didn't arrange it, then?'

'Me? I had nothing to do with it. It was my father
ho...' She stopped in mid-sentence and colour spotted
er cheeks. 'Look, if that's all you came here for——'

'Why?' He moved forward quickly, before she could
ıck away, and took her by the shoulders. 'Why did he
ant you to pretend I had hurt you?' His eyes darkened.
Ieaven knows I would never do that.'

'I—I told Sam that. But—but he had some crazy idea
at—that he could influence things in Jandara——'

'By destroying my reputation,' Khalil said, his voice
at.

'He knows it was wrong,' she said quickly. 'I swear
you——'

'But you wouldn't let him lie.'

Joanna's throat worked. 'I—I didn't think it was right.'

Khalil's hands spread across her shoulders. 'And so
u told two hundred million people that you went away
th me willingly.'

She felt the rush of crimson that flooded her cheeks. 'Please go now, Khalil.'

'Not yet, not until I have the answers I came for.'

'You have them. You wanted to know if my father and I——'

'I wanted to know why you told the entire population of the United States that you love me,' he said softly.

'It was—I mean, I thought it was——' She looked up at him helplessly. 'I couldn't think of anything else to say.'

He grinned. 'Really.'

'Yes. Really.' Joanna swallowed hard. 'I didn't mean it, if that's what you think.'

What he thought was that she was still the most beautiful woman in the world, and that he would surely have died if he had never looked at her wonderful face again. He smiled and traced the fullness of her bottom lip with his thumb. The last time he'd gazed into Joanna's eyes, his heart had been so filled with pain that he had been blind to everything but his own anguish.

But the passage of time had made him begin to wonder if he'd reacted too quickly that terrible morning three months before. He had dreamed of her for weeks, thought of her endlessly, and now he had come to the States on a mission for his country—but in the back of his mind, he knew he had come to find her, to find the truth...

...and there it was, shining along with the tears that had risen in her beautiful green eyes. He was certain of it, certain enough to do something he had never done before, put aside his pride—and offer up his heart.

'Didn't you?' he said softly.

Joanna swallowed again. 'Didn't I what?' she whispered.

'Didn't you mean it when you said you loved me?'

She closed her eyes. 'Khalil—please, don't do this——'

'I think the only time you lied about how you felt was that morning outside the cave.'

Her lashes flew up and she looked at him. 'You're wrong. I don't love you. I never——'

He lowered his head and gently brushed his lips over hers.

'How could I have been such a pig-headed fool? You told Abu you loathed me to save my life—didn't you, Joanna?'

Joanna stared into Khalil's wonderfully blue eyes. She could walk away from this with her pride intact. Well, sure, she could say, smiling, I did—but that doesn't mean I love you. I just did what I could to save your neck because it was the right thing to do...

'Joanna.' He cupped her face, tilted it to his, and when she looked into his eyes again, her heart soared. 'Beloved,' he whispered, 'will it be easier to tell me the truth if I tell it to you first?' Khalil kissed her again, his mouth soft and sweet against hers. 'I love you, Joanna. I love you with all my heart.'

Her breath caught. 'What?'

'Why do you think I kept you captive, even after I knew your father would never negotiate for your release?'

'Well, because—because——'

He smiled and put his arms around her. 'It was wrong, I know, but how could I let you go when I'd fallen in love with you? I kept hoping you would stop hating me, that you'd come to feel for me what I felt for you.'

Joanna felt as if her heart were going to burst with joy. 'Oh, my darling,' she whispered, 'my love——'

He drew her close and silenced her with a kiss. Then he sighed and brought her head to his chest.

'That night in the cave, I let myself believe you loved me, but the next morning——'

Joanna leaned back in his embrace and flung her arms around his neck. 'I do love you,' she said, laughing and weeping at the same time, 'I do!'

He kissed her again. After a long time, he lifted his head and smiled into her eyes.

'Lilia speaks of you. She is very happy. Her father was found alive, in one of Abu's dungeons.'

'That's wonderful!'

He grinned. 'Rachelle still speaks of you, too. She says she hopes some day you will see the error of your ways and admit what a wonderful person I really am.'

Joanna laughed. 'I'll do my best.' Her smile faded and she touched the tip of her tongue to her lip. 'Khalil— about Lilia. I felt awful, involving her in my escape, but——'

'Do you still have it in your heart to be a teacher, beloved?'

She looked at him with a puzzled smile on her lips. 'What do you mean?'

'There is much to do in my country. Lilia, and all the children, are eager to learn.' Khalil kissed her tenderly. 'Do you think you could give up your job at Bennetton and come back to Jandara with me to teach them?'

Joanna's eyes shone. 'Is that all you want me to do?'

'What I want,' he said, holding her close, 'is for you to be my wife and my love, and to live with me in happiness forever.'

As the sun rose over the Manhattan rooftops, Joanna gave Khalil her promise in a way she knew he would surely understand.

HARLEQUIN PRESENTS®

Harlequin brings you the best books, by the best authors!

Coming next month:

Harlequin Presents #1785
Last Stop Marriage by Emma Darcy

Award-winning author
"Pulls no punches..."—*Romantic Times*

Dan's wanderlust had spelled the end of his marriage to
Jayne...or *had* it?

But if he despised stability, how could he suddenly be a
daddy, and to *such* a cute baby?

Jayne found herself hoping that the last stop on Dan's
journey would be a passionate reunion...with her!

Harlequin Presents #1786
Dark Apollo by Sara Craven

"Ms. Craven does a magnificent job."—*Romantic Times*

Nik Xandreou *dared* to accuse Camilla's sister of being
a gold digger. So a furious Camilla set out to prove
Nik wrong! But in the clash of personalities that followed,
Camilla found herself hoping that Nik would win their
contest *and* her heart.

Harlequin Presents—the best has just gotten better!
Available in January wherever Harlequin books are sold.

brings you

How the West Was Wooed!

Harlequin Romance would like to welcome you
Back to the Ranch again in 1996 with our new
miniseries, Hitched! We've rounded up twelve of our
most popular authors, and the result is a whole year
of romance, Western-style. Every month we'll be
bringing you a spirited, independent woman whose
heart is about to be lassoed by a rugged, handsome,
one-hundred-percent cowboy!

Watch for books branded Hitched! in the coming
months. We'll be featuring all your favorite
writers including, **Patricia Knoll, Ruth Jean Dale,
Rebecca Winters** and **Patricia Wilson,** to mention
a few!

A family feud...
A dangerous deception...
A secret love...

DESTINY

by Sara Wood

An exciting new trilogy from a
well-loved author...featuring romance,
revenge and secrets from the past.

Join Tanya, Mariann and Suzanne—three very special
women—as they search for their destiny. But their
journeys to love have very different results, as each
encounters the irresistible man of her dreams....

Coming next month:

Book 1—*Tangled Destinies*
Harlequin Presents #1790

Tanya had always idolized Istvan...well, he *was* her brother,
wasn't he? But at a family wedding, Tanya discovered a
dangerous secret...Istvan wasn't related to her at all!

Harlequin Presents: you'll want to know what happens next!

Available in January wherever Harlequin books are sold.

UNLOCK THE DOOR TO GREAT ROMANCE
AT BRIDE'S BAY RESORT

Join Harlequin's new across-the-lines series, set
in an exclusive hotel on an island off the coast of
South Carolina.

Seven of your favorite authors will bring you exciting stories
about fascinating heroes and heroines discovering love at
Bride's Bay Resort.

Look for these fabulous stories coming to a store near you
beginning in January 1996.

Harlequin American Romance #613 in January
Matchmaking Baby by Cathy Gillen Thacker

Harlequin Presents #1794 in February
Indiscretions by Robyn Donald

Harlequin Intrigue #362 in March
Love and Lies by Dawn Stewardson

Harlequin Romance #3404 in April
Make Believe Engagement by Day Leclaire

Harlequin Temptation #588 in May
Stranger in the Night by Roseanne Williams

Harlequin Superromance #695 in June
Married to a Stranger by Connie Bennett

Harlequin Historicals #324 in July
Dulcie's Gift by Ruth Langan

Visit Bride's Bay Resort each month wherever
Harlequin books are sold.

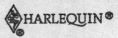

BBAYC

Harlequin Romance ®

brings you

Some men are worth waiting for!

Beginning in January, Harlequin Romance will be
bringing you some of the world's most eligible men.
They're handsome, they're charming, but, best of all,
they're single! Twelve lucky women are about to
discover that finding Mr. Right is not a problem—it's
holding on to him!

In the coming months, watch for our Holding Out for
a Hero flash on books by some of your favorite
authors, including LEIGH MICHAELS, JEANNE ALLAN,
BETTY NEELS, LUCY GORDON and REBECCA WINTERS!

HOFH-G

HARLEQUIN PRESENTS®

Ever felt the excitement of a dangerous desire...?

The thrill of a feverish flirtation...?

Passion is guaranteed with the seventh in our new selection
of sensual stories.

Indulge in...

Dangerous Liaisons
Falling in love is a risky affair!

The Sister Swap by Susan Napier
Harlequin Presents #1788

Acclaimed author of *The Cruellest Lie*

It began as a daring deception....
But Anne hadn't bargained on living next door to
Hunter Lewis—a man who wanted to know *everything*
about her!

Still, Anne managed to keep up her act for a while. Until she
realized that hiding the truth from Hunter meant that she
was also hiding from love!

Available in January wherever Harlequin books are sold.

DL-8